KU-161-043

The Cry of the
WOLF

By the same author:

An Angel for May
Burning Issy
Loving April
The Baby and Fly Pie

MELVIN BURGESS
The Cry of the
WOLF

Andersen Press · London

For Owen

First published in 1990
by Andersen Press Limited,
20 Vauxhall Bridge Road, London SW1V 2SA.
This edition published 2002.

All rights reserved. No part of this publication may be reproduced,
stored in a retrieval system, or transmitted in any form or by any
means, electronic, mechanical, photocopying, recording or
otherwise, without the written permission of the publisher.

Text © 1990 by Melvin Burgess.

The rights of Melvin Burgess to be identified as
the author and artist of this work have been asserted by him
in accordance with the Copyright, Designs and Patents Act, 1988.

British Library Cataloguing in Publication Data available
ISBN 1 84270 161 4

Typeset by Print Origination (NW) Limited, Formby, Liverpool.
Printed and bound in China

Chapter 1

Ben Tilley lay on the banks of the River Mole keeping very quiet. It was a still, hot day. The river moved silently below him and around him in the grass there were tiny rustlings and scratches from insects about their business. A robin was singing nearby and the sun beat down, baking into his back, pressing him into the dry mud. Ben could quite easily have fallen asleep if he had not been so excited.

Today was a bad and special day.

Ben was holding a gun in his hands. It had a wooden handle with a criss-cross pattern carved into it and bolted on with a thick, dull screw. The stiff little barrel was black and it was so heavy it hurt your wrist. He had found it in his father's garden shed and stolen it. It was not a real gun, only an air pistol, but it was still dangerous. It could shoot right through the shed door if you were close enough, and Ben thought you could kill someone with it if you got them in the eye. Certainly you could kill little animals and birds with it, and that was why he was lying so quietly on the riverbank. Ben was hunting water rats.

Ben was only ten and he had a lot of trouble keeping still. His breath seemed to clamour in the air around him. The drowsy riverbank was dangerous, and he was frightened and excited. When at last he spotted a little brown face he let off a long, quiet sigh - he had already scared two off - and carefully moved the gun round until it was pointing at the little animal. It sat there, wiping its whiskers in its perfect tiny paws, combing the neat fur on

5

its face, rubbing its eyes and peeping this way and that. Ben had it right in his sights now, but before he shot he couldn't help checking that no one was watching. He was lying there so quiet that it seemed impossible that anyone could creep up without him hearing, but even so he peered quickly over his shoulder. When he looked back, the water rat was gone.

'Oh...' he moaned quietly. The ordeal of being still again was too much when he was so excited.

The sun had pushed its way through his thick blond hair and was burning the back of his neck. When he half closed his eyes, the gun seemed to disappear and only the heat, the river, the robin singing hidden in the willows and the tiny rustlings of little insects remained - a peaceful sunny day.

Ben opened his eyes. A water rat was sitting on a ledge of mud opposite, a perfect target. It was cleaning its head like the first one, sitting up like a squirrel, busy and clean and neat, a little packet bursting with life. He did not make the mistake of looking round twice. This time he thought of nothing but hitting the little thing dead.

The water rat sensed danger, put its front paws onto the mud - too late. Ben fired - phhhussst - plop! - water rings crossed the river towards him; the water rat was gone.

'Not a very good shot, are you?' said a man's voice behind him.

Ben spun round, as if he had been shot himself. There was a little man standing there. He smiled slightly; his limp face made dimples. He had a neat moustache cut level and straight above his thin lip and his smooth skin and still face were damp and shiny. There was a small white dog with a lopsided face and crooked legs sitting next to his shoes. It sat crookedly, too, as if it was injured.

'It's my gun,' lied Ben. The man looked down at him and smiled and said nothing. Ben swallowed and wondered if he could just walk away. Nothing in the man's expression told him what was going to happen.

The silence was worse than being told off. 'Where did you come from?' pleaded Ben. And that was another thing. The day had been so quiet you could hear the beetles creeping in the grass. How had the man come up to him like that?

The man held out his hand. 'Give me the gun.' Ben handed it over. 'And the pellets.'

He loaded the weapon and looked down the sight. Then he fired it off into the bushes. 'It shoots to the left,' he remarked.

At the sight of the gun in her master's hand the little dog stood half up, and Ben saw that one of her front legs was shorter than the other.

'She's got the best nose of any dog there is,' the stranger told him. As he spoke he peered into the bushes opposite, moving his head this way and that like a cat. 'A hyena did that to her. She was following his scent and got so wrapped up she ran smack into the back of him. If I hadn't been right behind her, she'd have been dead meat.'

Ben looked up at him. 'Are you a hunter?' he asked.

For an answer the man fired the pistol into the bushes again. The little dog huffed and shuffled. 'Fetch it, Jenny,' he commanded, and she rushed off, dashed through the water into the bushes and came back a moment later with a dead sparrow in her mouth, which she laid across his shoes.

'That was a good shot!' said Ben grudgingly. 'And she must be a real hunting dog!' Ben didn't like this man, but he was very impressed. Anyway, there had been no mention of the police or his father, and he felt he ought to say something nice.

Now he wanted to see more. 'Do it again, get another one,' he pleaded.

The man reloaded and looked around him. He gestured to a clump of blackthorn bushes slightly downstream. 'See anything there?' he asked. Ben saw nothing. Again the man fired the pistol, again the little dog dashed crookedly off into the water and to the thicket. She returned with another little bird and laid it neatly next to the last one. The man nodded.

Ben looked down at the bird. Its beak was open and stained with blood. The feathers were untidy on the neck where the pellet had gone in, a little mess of bloody fibres. Its breast was red too, but not with blood.

'But it's a robin,' he said. As he spoke he realised that the birdsong bursting from the bushes nearby was now dead.

The man shrugged. 'Why should you feel sorry for a robin and not for a sparrow?' he asked. Ben shrugged. 'Because they're prettier?' asked the man with the hint of a sneer in his voice. 'That makes them more worth killing.'

'Did you really kill a hyena?' demanded Ben. 'Was it in Africa? Have you hunted lions?'

The man nodded again. 'I've killed lions, elephants, hyenas, hippos . . . '

'Rhinos?'

'Rhinos . . . tigers . . . '

'Tigers?' exclaimed Ben, out of breath with admiration.

'You've really killed tigers? How many?'

'More than anyone else I know of,' smiled the man.

'It's not true.' Ben started doubting the man again. He didn't know whether he was to be admired or hated. 'Tigers are protected, it's against the law to shoot them.'

'So are robins,' replied the Hunter.

'Are you going to hunt animals in this country?' demanded Ben.

The man waved his hand carelessly. 'There aren't any animals left worth killing over here.'

'You can hunt foxes,' said Ben.

The man sneered.

'You could hunt the wolves,' exclaimed Ben, suddenly.

The man looked at him in surprise. Everyone knew there were no wolves left in England. The last one had been chased and beaten to death five hundred years before.

'Who told you there were wolves here?' he asked.

The boy looked guilty, but just babbled on. 'My dad showed them to me. It's a secret. They come past our farm. Dad leaves out scraps for them sometimes but they never touch anything . . . There's lots of them . . .'

'Show me one,' said the man. 'And I'll kill it for you.'

Ben's face dropped. He looked shocked. The Hunter was amused. The child really did seem to believe in these wolves.

'If I find any wolves, I'll kill them. All of them,' he said, just to make it worse.

Ben shuffled. He looked close to tears. 'I've got to go now.' He stepped away but the man called him back.

'Aren't you going to take this?' He held out the gun and the pellets. The little dog at his feet yawned. Ben looked at the gun and said nothing.

'Shall I throw it away?' asked the Hunter.

There was a silence. Ben did not want to take anything from him - especially the gun.

'If it's yours,' went on the man in an unpleasant voice, 'I expect your parents will wonder what you've done with it.'

Ben shuffled forward and took back the gun and pellets. The man handed him the weapon but didn't let go. He raised his eyebrows expectantly. Ben could see his teeth shining dully, like the big screw in the gun handle.

'Thank you,' he said.

The Hunter let go of the gun. Without a word he turned and walked away, the crooked little dog at his heel, leaving the boy standing behind with the gun.

'Don't shoot any wolves with it, now!' he called over his shoulder.

Before he went home, Ben kicked the dead robin and sparrow into the water.

Chapter 2

The Hunter was on his way back from a business meeting and had only stopped off for a breath of air. As he walked back down the riverbank towards his car, his eyes automatically scanned the ground, looking for signs of animals. He turned his head slightly this way and that to pick up noises. It was so much a habit to track and look for clues of wildlife that he never stopped doing it, even when he had no idea of finding any game.

When he got back to his car he wanted to buy a few groceries, so he drove up to the village shop about half a mile away. There, he mentioned the boy he had met shooting water rats by the river and the shop woman recognised his description. She swore to tell his parents. Then the Hunter told her what Ben had said about the wolves, and to his surprise, she flushed and pursed her lips, looked shocked. For an exciting moment he believed there really were wolves to kill.

Outside in the sun again, the Hunter could not believe he had been so foolish. Wolves in southern England! And yet the way Ben had told it - and now this woman - certainly it seemed something was going on.

He recalled that Ben had mentioned that the wolves came near his father's farm. The shop woman had already given him the name. An enquiry from a passer-by got him directions on how to get there. He decided to drive along and have a nose about. Perhaps he would unearth something interesting.

It was only a short drive. He parked his car in a lay-by on

the main road and got out with Jenny to walk along the small road - almost a track - that led to the farm where Ben lived with his parents. The hedgerows were full of wild roses and buzzing with insects. It was late afternoon now and the air was heavy with the heat of the long, hot day, and thick and fragrant with the smell of the fools' parsley that grew in great white drifts by the roadside. Some way off he heard a dog barking regularly - one of the farm dogs, he supposed.

When he reached the farm he peered through the trees at the house. He could see Ben sitting on his own and mooching around the steps of the house. He looked fretful. The farmer was busy in an outhouse, banging something with a hammer and the sound of his hard work floated lazily out into the still air of the yard. Inside the house the telephone began to ring. The Hunter wondered if it was the shop woman, ringing to tell on Ben.

At a motion from her master, Jenny crept close to his heels and moved quietly and swiftly behind. Taking care not to be seen, the Hunter glided like a shadow past the farm buildings and on to where the little road became a dirt bridleway beyond. Once past, he relaxed and sauntered along the track, hands in his pockets, his eyes scanning the ground. Occasionally he paused to examine plants by the wayside, or marks in the damp edges of the track. To one side of the track was a small patch of woodland, beyond which was pasture leading up to more woodland. On the other side was a field planted with cabbages that led down to the River Mole. The sun was going down behind the hill, casting long tree shadows down to the river, and marking time across the bridleway with the long, thin sloping shadows of the fenceposts.

He came to a place where the remains of a flood-stream

ran along the pathway. Something here caught his eye and he bent for a closer look, moving his head to and fro as he scanned the mud. Then he got down on his haunches to examine the mark of a pad in the dried mud of a rut that had once held water. Jenny became still and watched closely as her master scanned the ground for more marks. He found a trace of mud on the greenery by the edge of the field and then waded through the thigh-deep grass and flowers to pick a few hairs from the barbed wire, where some golden-grey animal had squeezed underneath.

The Hunter looked out across the cabbage field to the woods above. He said, 'Wolf.' He turned and went back to examine the pug mark in the mud again. Sensing his excitement, Jenny crouched and wagged her tail warily.

'Wolf,' he repeated. 'Without any shadow of a doubt. Incredible.'

All his life the Hunter had killed rare and exotic animals. It did not matter if the beast was dangerous or not, or easy or difficult to track down. He did not care about sport. It only mattered to him that his prey was rare, and the rarer it was, the more glamorous the killing became. Above all it seemed to him a glorious thing to shoot an animal that no one else had hunted.

He remembered when he was a little boy reading a book about the last wolves in England. This book had the dates that the last wolves had died, where they had been shot and who had killed them. The Hunter thought that fame like that was the best thing in the world. To kill the very last remaining one. Someone had killed the last bear in England; someone had killed the last beaver. If you did something first, it could be done over and over again after you; but to do something last made you unique and famous, and the Hunter wanted that more than anything.

The Hunter examined the prints again. 'It must have escaped from somewhere,' he told himself. But he knew this was a real wild wolf. He had seen prints of wolves from all over the world and he knew that every kind of wolf had a slightly different print. These English wolves were different again. They were small and neat, the plump oval toes closely grouped around a distinctive clover-shaped central pad. He knew that this wolf was of a kind he had never seen before.

He called Jenny over to sniff the tracks. He closely examined the vegetation on both sides of the bridleway and then jumped the barbed wire into the cabbages. Jenny ran up and down the parched earth at the edge of the field, sniffing the ground between the few thin yellow weeds that had survived the farmer's weed-killer. Shortly, she set haltingly off in between the cabbages. The scent was old, man and dog made slow progress, frequently pausing to check the vegetation, or for the little dog to sniff up and down before she was sure of her way. The tracks were confusing, criss-crossing other tracks, doubling back and full of tricks. But they found their way across the field to the river. They splashed across and Jenny ran up and down a few times before finding the scent again. Quicker now that she was learning how the wolves ran, the little dog led the way across the pasture and off into the trees on the hilltop.

The last wolves in England, at the time the Hunter discovered them, numbered around seventy animals, running in seven separate packs. Over the centuries their numbers rose and fell, sometimes getting as low as forty, never rising higher than two hundred. They had lived a hidden life, forever on the run, on the verge of extinction for five hundred years and for much of that time no human being had known of them. A farmer or countryman might wonder what those odd dogs he occasionally saw about were doing. Only rarely someone guessed that they were really wolves, and the knowledge would be handed down for a few generations before it faded away again. In the small village where Ben lived, only a handful of people knew of the wolves. It was the Hunter's luck that he had met two of them on the same day.

How had they survived?

Their ancestors had come from the north of England, where the last English wolves lived, and had been chased with swords and pikes and scythes, with arrows, with dogs, with fire, and finally with guns. Their numbers had been picked off, one by one, family by family, until only the most cunning and careful of their race remained. Those few had been chased and hounded out of Cumbria, south into Lancashire, east to Yorkshire, and on again to the south. Every time they shook off one hunt, another would begin. This long hunt, in the end, took the last wolf pack so far south that they came to parts where no wolves had been seen or heard of for hundreds of years. The dogs had ceased to bark; they had forgotten the smell of wolf. Men had ceased to shout. Down in the countryside south of London, where the last wolves had been hounded to death centuries before, no one any longer knew what made a wolf. If anyone did see them who knew something of wolves, they soon dismissed the idea that wolves could be at large in this of all places.

But the wolves never forgot how dangerous Man was. Hundred of years had passed, but every one of them carried inside the memory of what the ancient cry 'Wolf! Wolf!' meant to them . . . the fire by night, the baying of dogs and the cruel, excited shouting of men and children. The chase, slithering across wet fields, scrambling over rocks, dashing between houses, until their lungs were bursting, stones striking their ribs and cracking their skulls, torches of pitch ablaze tumbling towards them . . . and then the killing . . . the smell of their own fur burning, of their flesh and bones sizzling and charring as their dens blazed . . . their cubs thrown up and broken and trampled on the ground, their blood running thick in the open air . . . sticks beating their hides until the bones broke and broke again . . .

They learned to be invisible. They never hunted domestic animals, but lived only on wild meat. If they came to a field with sheep in it they skirted round it. They were always on the move, never staying in the same place for more than a few days.

So successful had they been they had kept their secret for all these hundreds of years. Only now had they been betrayed and for the first time an outsider had discovered them.

Two nights passed before the Hunter came back to his car. It was raining and the cabbage field was sodden clay. He didn't go back to the track but cut straight across to the main road, kicking the clods of mud off his shoes as he walked and slipping occasionally under the weight of a burden wrapped in black polythene that he carried hunched over his shoulders. Jenny trailed behind him, bedraggled and miserable. He came out only a few metres

16

away from his car, still parked in the lay-by, and the light of a street lamp caught his face as he stepped over the wire. The chin was now stubbly, the skin was wet. There was no expression on his face, but it shone from within with a kind of delight.

He flung the burden down onto the muddy verge while he fumbled in his pocket for the keys. A corner of the polythene blew over in the wind and the face of his victim showed in the street lamp.

It was the same animal that had left tracks on the bridle-way. It was a dark coloured male wolf with golden hair around his face. Blood was drying between his teeth and dribbled slowly from his ear onto the grass verge. There was a neat round hole behind his ear. He was still warm. He had only been dead a few hours.

The Hunter wrapped the corpse in a blanket and put it in the boot of the car before he drove off for a hot bath and a drink to celebrate his first wild English wolf.

Chapter 3

On a still, frosty winter morning, three years after the Hunter had made his first kill, a large floppy labrador called Mike was out with his master for an early morning run. Trotting on ahead along the same path they took every morning, Mike turned a corner on the edge of a patch of common land and saw a strange dog. He stopped to have a good look. It was a tall, lean animal and it was behaving in an extremely odd manner, walking to and fro chest deep in long, dead grass, holding its chin in to its chest and looking down its nose as it walked. Then it suddenly leapt up as if it had been stung. Mike raised his eyebrows in surprise. The dog then shot down to the ground with a kind of straight-armed dive and snatched something out of the ground, before beginning its stilted walk in the long grass again.

Mike shook his head and looked again. He had never seen a dog behave like this before. He barked at it, but to his indignation the other dog barely gave him a glance. Mike stiffened and let off a whole series of good, loud barks, just as his master came round the corner, and then stood wagging his tail proudly with his nose in the air to see what effect his magnificent effort had had. But the other dog had gone. Mike looked suspiciously around him. When he realised that it wasn't behind him or to either side, he went over to have a sniff where the strange creature had been.

'Come on, Mike!' called his master cheerfully. Mike ignored him, and galloped and flumped over to the bracken. He almost fell over the other animal, who was

18

sitting hidden in the grass. Resignedly and with a hint of a sigh, it got to its feet and let Mike sniff it. Mike's master looked over his shoulder and saw his labrador sniffing a strange dog, a dog that gave him a curiously intense, almost alarming stare. He paused for a better look.

Mike backed off, full of suspicion. The new dog didn't smell right, somehow. He decided a game was the answer and crouched low, wagging his tail. The strange dog gave him a look. Mike tried an encouraging bark, but it came out all wrong. His tail dropped. He barked once more and began to growl, then thought better of it. Feeling a great fool all of a sudden, Mike backed off and then turned his back and trotted back to his master, trying not to skulk.

'Never mind, boy.' His master rubbed his ears for him. Mike huffed gratefully and glanced back disdainfully, if nervously, over his shoulder as they went round a corner. The other dog was already gone.

As he walked the man kept an eye out for rabbits or even a hare, if he were lucky. He would have been thrilled to see a fox that morning and delighted to see a badger. He did not know that he had just seen one of the rarest animals in the world. But then, he might not have felt so secure in his early morning walk had he known he was in the middle of a wolf pack.

The wolves were by now in danger of complete extinction. Their numbers were already so low that it was doubtful they could ever recover. Of the seven packs of three years before only one other remained, a group of six animals in hiding in the Forest of Dean in Gloucestershire. The Hunter knew where they were, he considered he could pick up their trail any time. First he was intent on wiping out this pack.

Three years before the man and his dog would have been surrounded by wolves, eleven of them. Now only four waited behind trees, hidden in the grass, under bushes, until he and his dog had gone.

As the man and his dog vanished into the morning mists, the wolf Mike had seen, a young female, rose from her hiding place and began her strange walk across the grass again. She was hunting mice, which made up a very large part of the wild wolves' diet. In half an hour she had caught fifteen - quite a good meal, even for a wolf. No dog would have thought of making a meal of mice; probably no dog could actually catch them.

The other wolves lay in a circle around her, watching out for people and other trouble. When the young female had finished she lay low and crept out of sight to a place under a thicket of gorse bushes where a beautiful cream and silver wolf lay resting on her side. This wolf was Silver, the pack leader. Her belly hung heavily on the icy ground. Silver was pregnant. Her cubs were due within the week.

When she lay by her leader's side, the young wolf began suddenly to heave and retch and then she spilled out half of her catch on the ground by Silver who quickly gobbled them up.

Her task over, the young wolf crept away and lay in the grass some way off. Further along the common, another animal rose from behind a crest of dead grass at the foot of an old fence, disturbing a flock of rooks poking for worms nearby. This was a short, stocky wolf, powerfully built with a fine golden ruff over his shoulders and around his neck. The golden blond fur spilled onto his face, like a mask.

This wolf, Conna, stalked up and down in the grass for

a while, but then seemed to get fed up with it and began rolling on his back instead. He paused and a look of surprise came over his face and then he began to squirm and wriggle in a most absurd manner, whimpering and groaning softly. There seemed to be something wrong with him.

The rooks in the field certainly seemed to think so, and began calling and croaking among themselves. Several of them stopped poking in the ground for worms and lifted their heads to get a better look. Others began walking towards the racket, making noises that might have been laughter. Conna certainly looked very absurd indeed.

Whatever was wrong with the wolf, it seemed to be getting worse. He began jumping up and down in the air, his tail thrashing and twitching. Then he lay still for a second before going into more spasms. He hunched over his stomach as if he felt ill, retched a couple of times and then began chasing his tail in ludicrous little circles, round and round.

The rooks gawped and looked at one another in amazement. A group of three jumped into the air and settled about twenty metres away to have a better look, and as Conna got more and more demented, they walked towards him, jeering and cawing, unable to take their eyes off this absurd beast. The rooks got closer and closer, Conna got madder and madder - but then, he suddenly leapt an enormous leap into the air and landed smack in the middle of them. The rocks squawked and flew off with a great clatter of wings, but it was too late for one of them. Conna had caught breakfast the easy way.

But it was not his breakfast. He too lay down on his belly and ran along the ground, so as not to be seen, and brought his gift to Silver under the gorse. The two wolves lay nose to nose for a second, giving each other long wet-tongued kisses, and hugging each other with their forepaws before Conna left to get his own breakfast. The two were mates. Wolves mate for life. Silver had been left a widow once before, because of the attentions of the Hunter. This was to be Conna's first litter, and he was as proud and as nervous as a puppy with its first mouse.

After Conna had finished his breakfast, it was time to be off. Silver rose heavily from her hiding place in the gorse. He ran to her side but at a low growl from her, sheered off. It was not good to stay too close together, in case of ambush. Silver shook herself before moving forward through the bracken and stubby gorse bushes, over the little stream and into a cow pasture beyond. One by one, her pack followed her.

It was winter, the deep frozen heart of January. The ground was hard as iron and the frosty grass brittle beneath their feet. The wolves moved quietly between the cows, ghosts from a past that England had long ago killed off and forgotten. The pasture led south over gentle hills to the farm and the stretch of river where, three years before, young Ben had told the Hunter that there were wolves.

That corner of Surrey where Ben's father raised crops and grazed cattle had been part of the pack's ground for centuries, and normally they would pass along the bridleway two or three times a year. But this was the first time Silver had led her pack this way since the Hunter's first kill – Goldface, Silver's original mate.

The murder of her Goldface - the first killing of a wolf any of them had known - brought swift action from the pack leader. She led them west through Sussex and then off their normal beat into Hampshire and then north right up into Wiltshire. The wolves had used every trick they knew to shake off the scourge that came among them, but even so the Hunter tracked down and killed three more before they threw him off and he picked up on another pack. Silver's pack had been saved, but the Hunter had soon appeared among another pack - then another - and another. The precious numbers of the wolves dwindled, slaughtered one after the other. Silver kept well away from her old haunts and wandered further north into Staffordshire. Here the pack was safe for three years, until at last a new animal had come up from the south to join her, the last member of another wolf pack. The Hunter had followed him. Now he was among them again, killing. And this time, after three years' experience, he was more dangerous than ever. So far Silver had been unable to shake him off their track. Only now had she led her wolves back into Surrey as she crisscrossed the southern counties in her efforts to shake him off.

Silver was very tired. The wolves had been moving fast for weeks. This was a race for her life, for the lives of her unborn cubs and the life of her pack. The Hunter was ferocious, cunning, with no mercy, no thought of reprieve. He wanted every one of these wolves dead by his hand.

Brindles, the oldest of them, and Cacoo, a cousin of Conna, had been the first, killed as they were drinking from a small pool in woodland south of the Farthing Downs in Surrey. One more, one of Silver's own daughters, had been taken on the edge of Tunbridge

Wells and another old wolf, aunt to Conna, had been wounded on the railway line to Brighton, and died a few days later. Another two, both young pups, had been killed only a few miles further on; they had been slowed down by the dying old wolf and the Hunter had used his chance well. The terrible chase continued. Silver tried everything she knew and more, but it seemed nothing could throw him and his crooked little dog off the trail. The Hunter had learned fast. He knew how the wolves travelled, how they rested and fed, all their habits, and had developed a terrible, uncanny instinct to predict which way they would go. Thus he was often able to follow them so far and then cut ahead so as to ambush them, appearing suddenly and slaughtering two or three before they even knew he was among them. For this reason, when Silver heard from her scouts sent back to keep track of him, that he had disappeared, she did not rejoice, but wondered instead how and when he would re-appear.

After crossing only two or three fields, Silver felt she had to rest again. She sniffed the air anxiously and whined slightly. Her weakness, as pack leader, put all of them in terrible danger. They had been running all night. She coughed and lay back down, signalling a period of rest. Two of the others in their hiding places sank down, sighed, put their heads on their paws, and tried to snatch a little sleep. The third, the yellow-tinted young female, stayed alert, on watch for danger.

Conna was unable to relax. He lay still, which was his duty, but his ears were up and he was listening not for the sounds of danger on the air, but for his mate, hidden behind the crest of grass. And in a few minutes, his suspicions hardened as he heard a whimper come from her hiding place. Quickly he was at her side, but again a warning growl sent him straight back to his own place. Silver was in labour.

It is the habit of wolves to give birth alone, so the others stayed away, but the news spread among them. The one remaining sleeper was put on the alert and all the wolves strained their senses anxiously for the slightest sign of danger. This was the most vital time of all for Silver and for them. Should any real danger threaten they would have to leave her.

A couple of tits peeped in the branches overhead. The wolves lay still as statues in the bracken. Soon, frost began to form on their coats. Silver, whose early labour had been brought on by the tremendous chase across country, struggled to bring her pups into the dangerous world.

A quarter of a mile away, unaware of the rare drama unfolding behind him, the man and labrador continued their walk. The dog loudly and wetly snuffed about for signs of rabbits, not that he could ever catch one. The man, who lived in a small house with too many people, enjoyed the empty air of the early morning. But he was not alone in the field. A few steps further on and he met another man with a dog. This man was short, rather plump, with a straight mouth like a line cut out in his bland face and a short, sharp moustache. He carried a strange bag over his shoulder and the small white dog at his feet looked as though it had at some time had an accident.

The two men nodded without a word as they passed, but then the newcomer turned and asked over his shoulder, 'I don't suppose you've seen a dog up ahead, have you?'

'What sort of dog?'

'A mongrel. Got a bit of husky in him.'

'I saw something like that - maybe a few hundred metres further on. Mike tried to play, but he wasn't having it. He was in the long grass on the common - you can't miss it. You'll have to watch your dog round here, though - there's sheep.'

The newcomer chuckled. 'She's a devil - but she knows enough to leave sheep well alone. Good morning.'

The Hunter turned away, the friendly smile on his lips remaining like a shadow, as if he had put it on for a purpose and now could not be bothered to remove it. He walked on. He had hoped to be well ahead of the wolves, but now it seemed they had speeded up. He had two options: to follow behind and take them that way, or to try and keep to his original intention by cutting across in front of them and ambushing them. Ambush was better - that way he had more hope of killing several animals. He decided to try for it. He guessed the wolves would make for the woodland on the hill overlooking the farm; it was their habit to stick to woodland cover as much as possible.

His mind made up, the Hunter turned off the path and moved quickly. Jenny followed, scampering and making queer little jumps over the icy tufts of grass. The Hunter paused, picked her up and tucked her away in his pocket. She was best out of the way. The killing sometimes upset her.

Within an hour and a half, the wolf pack had nearly doubled. Silver gave birth to three healthy wolf cubs, two females and one grey-blond male. She allowed herself a

26

soft yip, and in a second the other members of the pack were with her. They crouched low and licked Silver's mouth and sniffed at the little ones, and for a minute or two, the wolves of England played together, chased tails, boxed paws, were happy. Congratulations did not take long; they had been in one place for far too long already. As soon as Silver had given the pups their first feed, the members of the pack carefully picked up one mewing little mouthful each in their tender jaws. The wolves melted away into the bracken, and continued across the remaining fields to the woodland above the farm.

Silver could not know how close her unique race of silver and golden wolves had been brought to extinction. She did not know how precious the few remaining lives were. But she did know how precious her cubs were to her.

The little one she carried in her mouth did not take kindly to being carted about in so undignified a manner and he wriggled violently about to show it. He soon became so angry that Silver snorted in amusement and put him down on the frosty ground to have a good look at this loud and surly son of hers. The pup liked the cold ground even less than the air, and he nosed blindly about, looking for a teat to suck and a warm tummy to huddle up to, crying loudly. Silver snorted again and licked the pup's back. He responded by lifting his heavy, big head up and mewing ferociously at her. Silver huffed and then flipped him over onto his back with her nose, and began licking his stomach until he fell asleep, before picking him back up and continuing across the field. She crept under the hedge that marked the boundary of the woodland, slid through a thicket of aspens and emerged into the wider space between full grown forest trees.

She heard the soft and violent thud ahead of her twice. She looked up and saw movement before her as two wolves ahead fell out of sight and with one bound she swung into the aspens again. The sound of another bolt in the air came in the same second and there was a sickening bloody thud on her own shoulder. She gasped and dropped the cub, and although her heart wrenched, her instincts took over and she stumbled back through the brambles and bare branches on three legs, her left front leg pinned by a short bolt to her ribs. The smell of her own wolf blood hot on the frozen ground filled her nostrils and she ran blindly, scentlessly on until the pain took away her strength and she sank to the earth in a ditch on the edge of the pasture. The blood from her wound flowed freely, melting the frozen leaves in the ditch beneath her. She closed her eyes and lost consciousness.

She was awoken by pain moments later to find Conna above her, gnawing at the stubby bolt in her shoulder with his teeth, his muzzle bright red with her blood. A great bruise was spreading all around the wound. Conna did his best to remove the bolt, but it was not possible. Silver lay, whining under his efforts for a few minutes more. But then she climbed back onto her feet and staggered towards the scene of the ambush. Conna followed, frightened, whining at her. It was a cardinal rule never to return to the scene of a murder, when the murderer might still be there. But Silver knew her pack was finished. She had seen the two others fall. But her cubs were still alive. She was determined to rescue them.

The Hunter was pleased with his handiwork. He

jumped down from the tree and walked over to examine the wolves he had hit. The first animal, the young yellow-blonde female, was cleanly shot. He bent down to examine the skin and as he did so he heard a little cry from the grass around it. Bending down he found to his surprise a brand new wolf pup, still blind. At the noise, little Jenny, who had been hiding trembling in his pocket all the while, poked her head out to see, and sniffed towards it. She had once had puppies of her own. The Hunter gave the blind little thing his finger to suck and it squeaked crossly when no milk came. Then he wrung its neck, thinking to mount it in a family group for his study.

The other wolf, struck through the abdomen, was lying in a great pool of blood, but still gasping, at the last edges of its life. The animal's eyes rolled up at him as he stood there. Jenny yelped and ducked back down into his pocket as he finished the wolf off with his knife.

A movement in the grass alerted him to the second cub, and now it occurred to him there might be more about. He strangled this one too, and began to walk over towards the aspens, where he had wounded Silver, to see what he could find there.

He was no more than three metres away when the bloody head of the pack leader appeared suddenly from the aspens, seized another cub from the ground in its jaws and disappeared. With a curse the Hunter broke into a run. He saw the wolf on three legs between the trees, skidding and falling sideways, and he knew that she was badly wounded. Slashes of blood marked her way out of the woods and into the now frozen field above the farmhouse. The field had been roughly ploughed for the winter, and Silver stumbled over the ragged sods, slithered, almost on her belly, down the slope, leaving her blood smeared on the icy furrows. The Hunter let off a bolt at her but missed and ran on, reloading. He knew he could not lose her trail now.

In the yard of High Pond Farm, a thirteen-year-old boy was fixing a puncture on his bicycle. The bicycle was old and not used much. But that weekend he and his friends planned a trip to the sea. It was the first long trip Ben had been allowed to make on his own and the condition was that he should make absolutely sure his bike was road-worthy. The poor old thing had been untouched for months. The tyres were both flat and it squeaked. Ben was covered in oil. He was clenching his teeth as he held the inner tube in a bowl of icy cold water, trying to find yet another leak. A thin stream of tiny bubbles crawled up his red fingers. Ben groaned.

There was a noise behind him. The boy turned. To his amazement and horror a great animal was creeping on its belly across the farmyard. Its ears were laid flat' on its skull, its eyes rolled so far back they were three quarters white. Its lips curled far up its black gums and teeth. Every hair on its body was standing on end and it looked enormous. It left a trail of blood behind it, practically brushing by his legs as it crawled into the barn, and it made the most fantastic noise as it went, moaning and growling deep in its throat at the same time. A small grey baby animal mewed in its bloody jaws.

Then there was a second noise. The boy turned again and now there was a man standing in front of him, panting. It was a man he had seen before. His teeth were bared, his face was red and he was crouched up as if ready to leap. Cradled in his arms was a crossbow. He straightened up when he saw Ben. For a second they looked at each other and then the Hunter said, 'That's my dog,' and took a step forward. Ben moved in front of him. 'It's got my pup, didn't you see?' screamed the man. 'It's killing him!'

For a second, Ben paused. The monster had got something in its jaws, and its jaws were covered with blood. The man jumped forward and pushed him aside. But Ben knew that man; he saw the crossbow.

He grabbed at the man's arm and pulled him back. 'That's no dog - Dad, Dad, come quick!' he screamed at the top of his voice.

The Hunter snarled. 'Get away.' He shoved the boy viciously off, but the farmer was already coming out of the door.

'There's a wolf in the barn, wounded,' said Ben. 'He's hunting her. He's the one I saw before. He killed the robin.'

The crossbow in the Hunter's hand told the farmer everything.

'Get off my land!'

The Hunter grimaced and stepped back. 'I'll have you!' he growled, and ran out of the yard. John and Ben Tilley turned to look in the barn.

Chapter 4

Silver had not even managed to hide in the barn, but collapsed in front of a bale of straw, nosed the cub to her chest and could do nothing but wait and see. When the door opened she did not raise her head but rolled her eyes to the people coming towards her. She made no attempt to escape. Crossing the yard had spent her very last dregs of strength. Seeing Ben and his father instead of the Hunter, her tongue fell out and she closed her eyes, panting shallow, wheezing breaths that clouded the air.

To Ben, this wolf was a different animal from the monster he had seen outside. Then she had stretched right across the yard like a demon and could have crushed him in her jaws. This creature was shrunken, collapsed, pitiful. The little bolt sticking out of her bloody hide was causing her agony. The fur all around the wound was sodden with blood.

John Tilley motioned Ben to stay where he was while he went to examine the wound. The wolf growled weakly and tried to scoop her pup close to her, but then licked her lips and laid her head down. She made no further protest. The bolt was wedged between her ribs. John knew that bolt had to come out. The animal had already lost a lot of blood.

'Ben, fetch me water and antiseptic. Tell your mother what's happened. And bandages. Be quick!'

With Ben gone, the farmer turned to the grim job of getting the bolt out.

Half an hour later John Tilley came out of the barn and

locked the door behind him. Mrs Tilley and Ben waited for him.

'Is she going to be all right?' Ben asked.

'It's a bad wound. The bolt didn't pierce her lungs, that's one thing. We'll see.' Catching his wife's eye, he softly shook his head. He held out the bolt. 'Crossbow,' he said. 'Makes no sound, you see, and it's every bit as deadly as a gun. Vile.'

While his parents talked Ben went to the door and bent on his knees to peer through a crack. He could see the wolf inside, breathing weakly.

'I'm sorry,' he whispered through the crack. The cub was crying, and Ben promised in his mind that if anything should happen to the mother he would look after her young one for her.

Silver was fighting for her life. John Tilley called the vet in, a local man who knew the story of the wolves, and he treated her with antibiotics and bathed her wound. But she was very weak and within a day had developed a raging fever. John and Margaret Tilley did not expect her to last the night, but the next morning she was still there, bright-eyed, blazing hot and dry. Her pup suckled empty teats.

'He needs feeding with a dropper bottle every two hours, day and night. Even so he'll probably die,' said Mrs Tilley. 'Any volunteers?'

So Ben spent the next day sitting in the barn with the two wolves with a blow-heater on a cable from the house, an alarm clock, a dropper bottle and an electric bottle warmer some friends of his parents had used for their new baby's night-time feeds. He was worried that Silver would not like him handling her young one, but in her fever she knew nothing of what was happening. She lay all day with her muscles clenching into stringy chains, panting and groaning, opening her wound as she struggled in a bitter delirium. No one knew whether she was fleeing or fighting for her life in her dreams. Every hour they expected her to die, but somehow she held on, her tongue hanging out like dry leather, her sides shaking, her eyes sinking and burning blindly in her head.

When evening came, though, and he tried to take the cub away to bed, she became distressed. Even in the violence of her fever she would not be separated from her last remaining cub and she dragged herself across the floor after Ben, staining the straw with her blood. He had to put the cub back at her side.

It seemed Ben would have to spend the night in the barn if he was going to keep his promise to Silver. But there was more than one protective parent about. Ben's father and mother would not leave their only son alone with the wolf.

'She's a mother, she's trapped and wounded with her last cub, and she's a wild animal, not a dog,' said his mother. 'She might not understand you're only trying to help.'

Ben said nothing. He knew his parents would not leave the cub to die, and he also knew Silver would not be separated from him. There was only one possible answer.

In the end, the whole family had to sleep in the barn, buried under an enormous pile of quilts and sleeping-bags. Outside, where the cold still held the country fast in ice, a small high white moon shone on the frozen concrete of the yard. Inside, the Tilley family and the wolves slept snug and warm, people and beasts together for once. Every two hours Ben turned on the heater and stretched his arm through the icy air to the crying cub. Silver, still ignorant of everything, panted hoarsely and whimpered. Ben watched her thin breath cloud the air, short clouds that dissolved at once, and that at any second might stop altogether.

On one such occasion, Ben awoke to hear some beast sniffing around outside the barn door. He stirred and immediately the animal was gone. Evidently there was more than one wolf left. During the day, Mr Tilley left the barn door ajar in the hope this other one might run in where he could be trapped and kept in safety, but Conna was too wary and frightened of men to be tricked in that way, even though it meant being apart from his beloved Silver.

Conna was not the only beast out and about in the Surrey countryside. Reports came from the village that the Hunter had been seen, asking questions in the village, hanging around the lanes near the farm. When he heard this, Mr Tilley tied up the two farm dogs at the entrance to the yard every night and kept his shotgun and stick by his side, as he slept.

The frost still held. Every day at one or two the sun in a cold blue sky melted the hoar frost on the yard, but as soon as it dipped everything re-froze at once. By the third day, Silver's fever had still not passed. She was as thin as a stick, her condition seemed unchanged. Her breathing was as shallow and rapid as ever, her tongue as dry, her temperature as high. Only her wound changed, developing a crusty scab under the matted fur of her shoulder. She ate nothing. Occasionally she lapped a little water, but sometimes she could not do even that, and Mr Tilley had to pour it down her throat.

Soon, Silver had either to die or the fever break. The Tilleys were scared of her. They prayed she would live, but if she won her fight and came to surrounded by people, cornered with her cub in their hands, would she understand? And if she did would she run - or would she attack?

While Silver remained hovering between life and death, her son was growing like a balloon, almost visibly. The little thing was changing colour already. His eyes were smoky blue; only later would they change to the true wolfish amber. He was obviously going to be a handsome animal. He had his mother's silver scattered over his flanks and gold blond mingled in with it. From a distance this mixture was a silver grey, although it became more rich close up, and Ben christened his adopted puppy Greycub. He felt he was doing something to make up for letting out the secret all those years ago.

'Stupid little kid,' he muttered to himself every night as he fed the precious cub. Ben knew that no wolves had been seen around the village for years - ever since he let the secret out, in fact. No one had ever accused him, but no one needed to. Ben guessed that the Hunter had been after the wolves all that time. How many had he slaughtered, unseen? Perhaps these were the last wolves left in England.

On the fourth night Ben awoke at the alarm that marked another feeding time. Full of sleep, he only vaguely noticed that something was different and was not aware that the short, jagged breath of the mother wolf was gone. Not until he reached out an arm for Greycub, and the air was cut by a low but very fierce warning growl, did he know that Silver was out of danger - and he was deeply in it.

Immediately his father and mother were awake.

'Don't touch him, Ben,' said his father.

At the sound, the cub had fallen immediately still, and there was no noise but for that growl, that said plainly, 'Don't' and seemed to come from all around them at the same time.

Ben already had the bottle in his hand. He moved it very slowly over to the cub. At once the growling flared up, threatened. His father turned on the lamp and Ben could see that the wolf was gone from her place and there was no sign of her. He could not work out where the growling came from. But his hand completed its journey, and Greycub began to feed. The growl continued, and went on after the bottle was empty and the light was out. Silver spoke her warning, but made no move. She wanted them to know she was there, she was watching, she was prepared to fight if need be for her cub.

It seemed as if she would never fall silent. No sleep was possible with that hair-raising threat all around them. But at last she stopped it and the occupants of the barn fell asleep. Greycub cried for her warmth, but Ben did not dare touch him and Silver remained in hiding.

The whole performance was repeated again at the next feeding time, but when they all awoke in daylight, Silver was back in her place by her son, and had shown the first signs of trust. Mother and son would live after all.

Silver began a slow recovery. She crouched all day, all bones among the straw, clearly uncomfortable at the human presence all around her, but accepting it as a necessary evil. Greycub had no such worries. He was fat and glossy and bursting with health and curiosity.

He spent his first weeks sniffing everything, measuring smells and sticking his nose into the air as soon as the barn door was opened, and the world was wafted inside on the freezing air. Once his eyes opened and he discovered things had shapes as well as smells, he wanted to be everywhere. Silver had no strength to amuse her cub and Ben had to keep him off her back. At first she was reluctant, but Greycub needed the exercise and soon she was glad to let Ben take over. The day she let her son sit on his chest and lick his face was one of Ben's proudest. As he got older, the cub developed the energy of a fireball, and just wanted to play all the time he wasn't eating or sleeping. Ben always ran out of energy first, running the little thing in circles or playing tag or just letting him ferociously try to chew his leg off.

Before long, Silver was able to trot around the barn. It was obvious from her sniffings at the door and scratching late at night, when she thought Ben was asleep, that she wanted to be off. Her milk had not returned, and if she did get away with her cub, Greycub would certainly die.

Now that Silver trusted Ben, and since no new sightings of the Hunter had been made for several weeks, Ben's parents returned to their bedroom, with every sign of relief. Although at first they had slept well in the open air, the frequent feedings had at last worn them down, especially Ben's father, who had to work long hours. So Ben was able to sleep on his own with the wolves.

He lay every night in his sleeping–bag among the straw and hay that made a bed for him and the two wolves. Silver had come to trust him so far as to lie against him, or even to rest her head on his legs as he slept, and Ben prized this trust more than anything.

By his side he kept a quartz clock that woke him at feeding times. This clock bleeped and then was silent for a while before bleeping again, and this way you woke up gradually. One night about six weeks after the wolves had come back to High Pond Farm, Ben awoke in the silence, thinking it must be time for Greycub's milk. He began to reach out for the bottle. But then he felt a breeze on his face.

A pale light from a small crescent moon and the dull electric farmyard light showed through the open door. There was a figure hunched over, arms gathered up to its face. Then there was a whizzing noise and a hard thud and a thin scream cut short came from behind him among the straw bales. Ben shouted and reached for his torch. In the sudden beam he caught the Hunter, hunched over his crossbow, raising his hand to shield his eyes. Ben screamed for help and reached out to the wolves. Silver was gone, but his hand caught the cub and he snatched at him. Just as the Hunter moved towards him, something big ran in behind and jumped right up onto the man's shoulders.

It was Conna. In the torch beam, again the wolf seemed to Ben to be enormous, at least twice as big as the man he was attacking. His huge jaws opened wide and he seized the Hunter's scalp with a terrible moan, and for a second Ben thought he would actually bite the man's head off. A second later the great beast dropped lightly to the ground and was gone.

The Hunter cursed and ran to Ben to seize the torch from him. Ben was screaming for his mum and dad, but he was shut up with a blow across the face and pushed to the back of the barn while the Hunter searched about. When he returned, he shone the beam in the boy's face.

Ben cringed in the light of the beam. He was still carrying Greycub under his arm.

'I'll have that,' growled the Hunter. He snatched the cub away and ran out of the barn. By now Mr Tilley was on his way but the Hunter pushed past him and in seconds had disappeared. The whole thing was over in two minutes.

Ben flicked on the electric light to the barn and together they searched for the source of that scream of pain that had come from behind. There they found one of the farm cats with the stubby crossbow bolt through its mouth and poking out of the back of its head. In the dark the Hunter had mistaken its eyes, glowing in the farm-yard light, for those of Silver. The two farm dogs, Bell and Clapper, that Mr Tilley had tied up to bark an alarm, were found outside still chained to their kennels, both dead, with crossbow bolts through their heads. The Tilleys searched high and low that night with torches and again the following morning, but of Silver, of Conna and of Greycub they could not find the slightest trace.

Chapter 5

As soon as he heard John Tilley out in the yard, the Hunter thrust Greycub into his coat pocket and ran as fast as he could down the track to his car, waiting on the main road. Trying to toss the crossbow over his shoulder he slipped and skinned his hands on the iron-hard frozen earth. He scrambled to his feet, cursing his luck. In his pocket, Greycub whined and he cursed the cub, too. It was a poor substitute for the two dead wolves he had promised himself for that night's work. Well, at least the two wolves were on the loose now, and he could get at them again.

It was three o'clock in the morning. The roads were clear and the Hunter raced his car south back home. In the back seat, Jenny crouched low, keeping well out of his way. The Hunter had not counted on the boy being in the barn. The brat had put him off, and given that monster the chance to attack. Why, the child was lucky not to get a bolt through his helpful little neck! And how could his parents be so irresponsible as to let their son sleep with wild animals - dangerous animals at that, as the wounds on his head and face showed.

In fact, the wounds were minor. He examined them in the car mirror and couldn't believe that the skin was broken in only a few places. From the noise that brute had made, he thought his whole scalp had been torn off, and he was badly shaken by the experience. The wolf could have killed him - it certainly had the chance. But so deeply ingrained was the wolves' instinct to leave humans alone, that Conna had been unable to do any real damage.

41

It had taken the complete breakdown and destruction of the pack to persuade him to touch the Hunter at all, and give Silver the seconds she needed to run past.

The Hunter lived in a small farmhouse on the Sussex Downs, a house he had bought when he found out that there were wolves thereabouts. He did not dare begin tracking Silver and Conna just then, now that the alarm was up. Best to go back home, get some sleep and pick up the track the next night while it was still fresh.

He was about halfway home when a disturbance in his pocket reminded him that he had something else to sort out, and he pulled into a lay-by to examine his night's prize. Greycub was trying to crawl out, and the Hunter looked down at the blunt puppy-nose and pricked ears, and the small bright eyes, peering cautiously under his pocket flap. The cub crawled right out onto the seat and seeing the Hunter, hunched his back and began a peeping growl, that was evidently supposed to be fierce. Unsmiling, the Hunter watched him.

He decided not to wring Greycub's neck. He thought the cub might come in handy later in tracking down Silver and Conna. Also, he might make a pet of him. So far he had told no one about the wolves or of his hunt. He wanted to make sure all the wolves were his. But when there were none left, then he would enjoy telling his hunting friends the stories of the three-year hunt. How much more telling these stories would be if he had a live wolf sleeping with its head on his feet while he described how he had killed off its entire race.

Greycub was growing up fast, but he still needed his milk and a mother. The Hunter knew of a man who lived nearby, who bred pedigree deerhounds for a living. There was a chance he might have a bitch in milk...

He tossed the cub into the back seat with Jenny and drove home. He would take the cub to the Breeder's first thing in the morning - if it was still alive, that is.

In the back, little Jenny remembered her own pups from years past and nosed the cub against her tummy and began to lick him clean. She paused and licked her lips for a moment, curling them at the strange taste, before she carried on with the wash. Greycub cried for milk before at last the little dog's tongue lulled him to sleep.

' - Found him abandoned in a car park. Someone obviously didn't want the pups and didn't have the guts to deal with them himself,' the Hunter said smoothly. The cub draped over his hand looked curiously about, letting out little peeps of distress. It was nine in the morning and he had been without milk for far too long. The Breeder looked doubtfully at him.

'I thought it was too much just to let him die like that,' continued the Hunter, 'and anyway my niece wants a pet so I thought I'd pick him up. I was wondering - hoping - you might have one of your deerhound bitches in milk with a teat to spare for him...?'

The Breeder did not like the Hunter. There was something about the way he spoke that was difficult to trust. This rescue of a dying pup was out of character. But the Breeder was a man to assume the best and this was the first time the Hunter had shown any sign of seeing animals as other than things to kill. He took the pup.

'I've got just the thing - a mongrel bitch, actually, I keep her for the better milk. The pedigree animals aren't so good for milk, you know. We'll see if she'll take him.'

43

He led the way into the kennels and to a small room round the back where, on a heap of sacks, lay a black and white dog. Cuddled up to her belly were three pups - two of her own and one young deerhound that the Breeder had taken from a mother with too many pups. Now he stroked the animal's head; she wagged her tail and licked her pups proudly.

'There's a girl - good girl,' the Breeder said. 'She's a gem, this one, she'll take anything. I could suckle wolves off her and she'd love them like her own, wouldn't you, girl?' He patted her on the head and held out the young Greycub for her to sniff. She wrinkled her nose, puzzled at the smell. But she did not object. She knew the smell was not dog, but she did not know it was wolf. Generations ago every hair on her body would have risen. Now she just looked up at the Breeder for reassurance. The Breeder tucked the pup up to a vacant teat. Immediately he began to suckle.

'Look at that!' he said in surprise. 'He'll live, that one. He's a fighter.'

The Hunter smiled. 'That's very good of you, my friend, very good indeed. Here . . . ' He took out his wallet and handed over a twenty pound note.

'That's to take care of any expenses until he's weaned. Then I'll come and pick him up.'

'No, please - it'll cost nothing . . . '

'I insist. You see, I've taken quite a fancy to the little fellow, I just want you to take good care of him, that's all.'

As the Hunter drove back home to get some more sleep before the hunt began again that night, the clouds overhead were beginning to darken. The cold spell was softening. From his bedroom window, Ben Tilley watched the same clouds and thought that somewhere out there, maybe Silver and Conna were sniffing the air and wondering if rain would come.

That afternoon the wolves had their first piece of good luck for a very long time. The frost had broken. It began with snow, but soon the snow was slush and then an icy rain began to fall. Ben, looking with a tearful face out of the window, was soon facing a curtain of rain, a flood, a torrent. Water bounced high into the air from the farm-yard and overflowed the gutters on the barn roof. A stream began to flow over the frozen bridlepath beyond the house, and quickly thickened into a river. Soon this river overflowed the bridleway and poured into the farmyard itself, carrying so much old moss and old leaves and twigs that the drains were clogged in minutes and Mr and Mrs Tilley had to dash out in rubber boots to clear them out for fear of the house flooding.

Ben pitied the wolves out in this weather, but the stream that flashed past the gate carried not only moss and twigs and old leaves but the trails and scents of the two wolves. The ground for miles around was washed clean of all scent, all tracks. When the Hunter came back he found the earth a clean blank page which was impossible to read.

Chapter 6

Human beings use their eyes to know the world. For dogs and wolves it is different. They know things and remember things not by what they look like, but by how they smell, and the very first things a young wolf or a young dog learns of the world about him come through his nose. It was smells that led Greycub by the nose out of the little puppy-world of milk and mother,· and into the big, million-scented world - into the hessian world of the pile of sacks he lay on, the smells of hay and straw from the bedding all around him, of disinfectant and wet metal as the kennel staff cleaned out - and the smell of the staff themselves, all soap and sweat, with their dinners and cigarettes on their breath and their clothes full of washing powders and fabric softeners, their skins carrying aftershaves and perfumes, a thick custard of chemical smells. He caught strange, exciting whiffs of the fresh air behind the kennels - the grass and the damp mud, the occasional rank puff of exhaust smoke. There were the meaty smells of the dogs' food, the smell of their water. There were the smells of the tiles on the kennel floor, of the wooden boards in the passage that led to the house, and the hot metallic smell of the electric heaters that kept the place warm.

Above all there was the smell of dogs. His mother's milky, warm, doggy smell, the doggy smell of all his foster-brothers and sisters, the smells of the forty deer-hounds the Breeder kept - all of them different, but all of them doggy, with doggy breath and coats, paws, wet doggy eyes and noses.

46

For a young dog, growing up among the smells of his own kind, this reassuring wind of their own dogginess is the first door to knowing who and what they are. Surrounded by an atmosphere of dog, they are dog themselves, inside and out.

For Greycub the wolf, this was not so. Inside the doggy bubble was another smell. It was similar in many ways, but there was no doubt that when his nose turned from the world outside into himself, he found something different. The world was not made up of animals like him. In fact, it seemed that there was nothing else like him around. The pressing bodies of his foster-brothers and sisters were too close and too warm to allow him to feel lonely. But already he was marked apart. He did not quite belong. He knew it, and the other pups knew it.

The pups were all slightly older than Greycub, but they were all interested in the same things - fighting, ambushing, growling, playing tag and being ferocious. The wolfcub was better than all of them at these games. After all, for wolves it is life or death; no one feeds them out of a can. But it was all good fun, and to start with he was more or less one of them, even though he smelt strange. But when the pups began to develop their doggy language, their vocabulary of growls and snarls and squeaks, it became clear that something, somewhere was wrong. Greycub found himself outside their culture.

Now, he began to keep himself to himself, or to wander off on expeditions of his own. Sometimes the kennel staff would try to play with him. He tolerated this, but allowed no liberties. The Breeder was different. Greycub decided early on that this was the one in charge, and he allowed him and him alone to roll him on his back and tickle his tummy, or to throw him up in the air. Anyone else was warned off with his most frightful growls and indignant yelps. Greycub could not understand that the other pups allowed just anyone to treat them like that. The silly oafish little things had no sense of dignity, he thought, and no sense of danger, either, come to that. He could never be like them.

In the middle of so many, Greycub spent his first few weeks alone.

One day in Greycub's tenth week, the Breeder came through to his corner of the kennel with another smaller man by his side. Greycub was too young to remember the Hunter, but some sense alerted him. He withdrew quietly and sat down on his mother's foot while the two men talked above his head.

'There he is, right as rain. A strong little fellow all right,' the Breeder was saying. 'But he's the strangest thing I ever came across. Look at him watching us. I tell you he won't let anyone near him but me - and even I can't take liberties with him. As proud as a little prince! You wouldn't think he's a dog, he's more like a wild animal. Even his foster-mother doesn't know what to make of him - look!'

The mongrel sheepdog, seeing all this attention to her ward, began to lick him possessively. Greycub put up with this for a while and then tottered off on his big feet out of reach. He growled when she tried to pull him back and she had to hold him down with one foot before he put up with it. He stared up at the two men curiously, disregarding his foster-mother as she licked

48

his belly.

'A bit of a loner,' commented the Hunter.

The Breeder reached down and picked Greycub up. He hung passively in the man's big hand and looked again, curiously, at the Hunter. The Hunter returned his stare and reached out to ruffle his head.

'Watch it! There . . . ' The Breeder laughed as the Hunter snatched away his hand and cursed. 'I told you - I'm the only one who can touch him. Strange, isn't it? It isn't as though I spent much time with him or anything. Even I'm not as popular as I was. A couple of weeks ago he'd have wagged his tail and been pleased to see me.'

'Strange,' said the Hunter.

'It is, isn't it?' said the Breeder. 'Look, I'll tell you what - I've come to get quite fond of the little thing - don't know why. He interests me. You don't know what sort of breeds are in him, do you?'

'No idea,' murmured the Hunter. 'I told you - I found him in a car park.'

'Anyway, what say I hang on to him? I'll give you one of the other pups for your niece - I don't suppose it'll make any difference to her, and he isn't exactly playful, is he? Hardly a dog for a little girl.'

'I'd rather not,' said the Hunter, firmly. 'As I said, I've got an interest in this chap.'

'Come on!' protested the Breeder. 'I'll tell you what - I want him. I'll give you one of the pedigree pups, how about that? Little girl with a deerhound - she'll be the terror of the street!'

'No,' said the Hunter. 'I want him. I'm sorry. I have reasons. The journey I was on when I found him was important to me.'

'Oh, well, if he means something to you . . . ' said the Breeder regretfully.

'Call it sentiment,' said the Hunter.

Chapter 7

While Greycub was weaned with the Breeder, the Hunter had been tracking down the one remaining wolf pack in Gloucestershire. He had been completely successful, as he was accustomed to be. Six bodies lay in the deep freeze, awaiting the time when he took them to be skinned and stuffed or turned into rugs, mementoes of the great hunt.

Silver and Conna were still free. He had no idea where they were. These two, together with Greycub, were the last wild wolves in the whole of Britain.

The Hunter had tried his hardest to find Silver and Conna in the past few weeks. Together with Jenny he had criss-crossed the area all around High Pond Farm, and then further afield all around that corner of Surrey. They had walked a great loop along the county borders, but they found nothing.

The cub offered the Hunter his only hope. True, weeks had gone by. Greycub had been living with men and dogs for so long that he no longer smelt of the wolf pack and quite likely Silver would no longer recognise him. Still, beneath the stink of dog and dog food, he was Silver's own flesh and blood, and pure wolf. If only the Hunter could get the two wild wolves to contact him in some way he might have a chance of finishing them off. Quite how he was to do this he did not yet know. He considered walking Greycub around the countryside, to leave his scent as far and wide as possible, in the hope the wolves might pick it up. Or he might let the cub go and hope it would take him to them. The cub was his only link with the wild wolves and he did not mean to be parted from him for a moment.

Greycub was growing fast out of his cubhood. His memory of the wild had faded, all but disappeared. It seemed to him that he had grown up with dogs and the mystery of his own strangeness was not solved by occasional ideas that once, long, long ago, there had been another life that in a strange way seemed more familiar than the one he now knew.

He had vague impressions of a terrible night when something happened that severed him from his own past, but he did not actually remember the Hunter. All he really knew had been the kennels; but still, he somehow recognised that the Hunter was an enemy, a man not to be trusted, not to obey - a man to resist.

His first instinct was to slip away as quietly and as quickly as he could, without the Hunter noticing. By the time the Hunter had driven home he was quite out of sight, and the man had to search the car before he found him sitting under the driver's seat. Inside, in the kitchen, while the Hunter turned his back to prepare some food for him, the same thing happened. When the man turned round he had disappeared, and it was over half an hour before he was discovered, buried under a pile of shoes in a cupboard under the stairs. He snarled and went for the Hunter's hand when he grabbed at him.

The Hunter was cross by now. 'Stay in one place,' he growled, and snatching Greycub by the scruff of his neck, he flung him into the kennel, a small utility room at the back of the house where Jenny slept. He pushed the bowl of dog food in after him and slammed the door shut.

Greycub knew with one sniff that this was a dog room and one glance told him that there was nowhere to hide. The room was empty except for a basket and a pile of blankets in the corner. He sniffed cautiously at the dog food, but decided it was too early to be sure anything was all right to eat in this place. He began to whine, but then thought better of it. It might bring the man back.

Then there was a movement in the pile of blankets. Greycub blinked and looked again - and a small white head with a crooked jaw poked out and looked at him. Greycub sniffed in its direction. This was clearly the owner of the room, and Greycub sank down submissively. After all, it was her room, and he was the interloper.

Jenny climbed out of her blankets and came to have a closer look, the hackles on her legs upright. She knew this smell. This was a wolf, and wolves were to be killed. On the other hand, although Greycub was now every bit as big as the little dog, he still had his great big feet and fluffy fur, and was still just a puppy. Perhaps Jenny remembered keeping him warm in the back seat of her master's car a few weeks before. Her motherly instincts were as strong as ever, and for the second time she began to lick the cub. Greycub sighed and sat down. Why did these dog things always want to lick? It would have been different, perhaps, if it had not been such a doggy tongue he was always being licked with. But he was glad he had one friend anyway.

After she had washed him, Jenny insisted that he eat and then led him back to the blankets. Rolled up together, the two dozed through the afternoon, dog and wolf cub. Every now and then, Greycub tried to snuggle closer to his new foster-mother, and he was so big he almost pushed the little thing off the blankets. But Jenny was happy; at long last she had something to mother, even if it *was* a bit big, and even if it *did* smell of wolf, and she kept nuzzling him with her nose, just to make sure he was still there.

Later that day, when he came in to let them out for an evening run, the Hunter was surprised to see Jenny ordering Greycub about, and him doing exactly as he was told. Another man might have laughed to see the tiny little thing trying to mother something bigger than herself. The Hunter however was only disappointed that Greycub had not accepted him as his new master, although he was gratified that through Jenny, he now had a way of getting the cub to do his will.

That night, left in the kennel with Jenny, Greycub awoke to see the moon shining through the only window in the room, a small, barred, single pane high up near the ceiling. In the kennels he had often woken up at night. It seemed to him part of his strangeness that when the dogs curled up and slept, he wanted to be up and running.

Without waking Jenny he left the blankets and went to sit under the window. It was slightly open and he could smell the night outside. Away from the kennel, which was the only home he could remember, Greycub now felt more alien than ever. Now, the full sense that he was alone in the world came to him, and for the first time in his life he tipped back his head and spoke in his own voice - he howled a true, wild wolf's howl. Immediately, Jenny was awake, growling and baring her teeth. Although she had never heard it before, she knew this was no dog song. The wolves of England had long ago learned to keep their music still; it was too dangerous to speak like a wolf in a world that would destroy them if it could. Greycub, separated from his kind, had no one to tell him that song was forbidden, and so he spoke, and wolf-song rolled over the Sussex Downs as it had not done for hundreds of years.

Up on the first floor, in a small room that was quite bare except for a narrow bed and a small chest of drawers, the Hunter was woken up. He lay in bed listening to the hollow, moving cry filling his bedroom and sailing out into the valley. Then he got up and walked across the thin carpet that lay directly on the bare boards, over to the window looking out across the hills.

The wide shallow valley unfolded itself into the darkness, revealed here and there by a few village lights, or a splash of moonlight on the fields and hedges. Out there were two wolves, the very last two - the ones the Hunter wanted most of all. In a way, he had killed all the others just to have this pleasure - the pleasure of killing the very last wolves in the country.

Greycub's cry spread and filled the valley, overflowed up to the horizon. The Hunter knew that if his prey were within a few miles of the house, they would hear and they would come.

Chapter 8

Greycub and Jenny spent their nights curled up in a ball
together in the kennel. The door to this was a slide door,
unlocked, but neither animal had the strength to push it
aside, so they were stuck there until the Hunter came to
let them out for their morning run. In one corner there
was a basket, but Jenny preferred to scratch the blankets
into a heap and sleep there. Greycub lay under her
chin.

Jenny had taken the cub completely under her charge.
She was wary of letting her master near him as if she
sensed he meant Greycub harm. But it was she who
made sure he did not run off when they were let out,
who took him into the kennel at night. She mothered
him to the point of fussiness, as if her own lost pups
were all somehow tied up in this one great big, strange
young creature. She became frantic if he went out of her
sight, fretted and worried that he finished his food and
lived in dread of him being taken from her, like her own
pups. She did all this in a furtive, guilty fashion, as if
she wasn't quite sure if it was all right. She began to
crouch and cringe, wagging her tail desperately whenever the Hunter came near, trying to placate him, since
she knew that creatures which smelt like the cub usually
meant a killing, and she spent endless hours licking and
washing him with her tongue, in a vain effort to make
him smell more like a dog and less like prey.

In the middle of a very dark and moonless night a
couple of weeks after the Hunter took Greycub back,
Jenny awoke to find herself alone among the blankets.

Greycub was sitting alert in front of the window, his head to one side, listening. She whined anxiously, calling him back to bed. Greycub cast a quick glance but took no notice. The little dog went to him, licking her lips and crouching, very unmotherlike, begging him to come back, almost as if she sensed he was passing beyond her.

Greycub stretched his jaws and shuffled tensely. He lifted his nose up to the window and sniffed.

Jenny sniffed the air, pricked her ears, turned her head this way and that, but sharp though her senses were, she could pick up nothing. The wolfcub, too, seemed to lose whatever it was that had been exciting him and he began to pace up and down the wall, sniffing aimlessly in the corners, whining fretfully. Then out of the darkness came a sound that Jenny recognised. She began to cry and beg again.

A long, musical wail floated across the garden, getting closer. This was no dog talk. The wolves were coming.

Upstairs a door banged. Feet rattled on the stairs. Greycub threw back his head and answered the call of his kind with his own true voice. The kennel door opened and he tried to squeeze through but a foot kicked him back.

'That was no dog.'

The Hunter clenched his fists. 'You've been worth your weight in gold,' he told Greycub.

Now the call came again and as the Hunter dashed out again, Greycub and the wild wolves called to each other as if they did not care if the whole world heard them.

Minutes later, fully dressed and with his bow over his shoulder, the Hunter called for Jenny and left the house. The little terrier followed him unhappily, looking back over her shoulder at where Greycub was still trapped inside. The howling outside had stopped now, but the Hunter had noted where it came from - about a quarter of a mile away, near a place called Tulley's Wood.

'Tonight I'll see the end of it,' he thought.

Greycub pushed against the door as soon as the Hunter and dog were gone, but he could not budge it. He turned back to the window and whined, stood up on his hind legs, yelped and howled, as if he expected something to come flying through.

He did not know what was happening or what to expect. That howl and a slight scent that a breeze carried in excited him to the point of fear. Out there, in a world he did not remember lived a creature that was a part of him.

Once the Hunter had left the house there were no more howls. Greycub grew despondent. He lay down on the blanket and sniffed the smell of Jenny, but it brought him no comfort. He was confused and miserable, relieved and terrifed at the same time that the mysterious, magic presence had gone. After ten minutes or so of crying, he buried his head under the blanket and went to sleep.

It was a scent that awoke him. This scent was brief but it was not pale or distant. In a second he was wide awake. Every hair on his body stood on end and he cringed down into the blanket, terrified and amazed that his own scent, transformed into something fierce and magnificent, should be stalking across the garden outside towards him. That one wall, that thin impenetrable layer of stone blinded him and cut him off from this great mystery, but the scent came thick and powerful through

58

the little open window above; it filled the kennel and flattened him to the ground.

At last, just a metre away on the other side of the wall came a small dry noise. The cub sprang up and hurled himself at the wall, whining and yelping, cringing and jumping up in turns, desperate to reach the presence so near, yet terrified of what he'd find. A second noise, a soft cough, and he had a vow of silence clapped on him. Instantly he crouched. That noise, which he had never heard before, was a warning to be still and although every nerve of him screamed to jump up he lay tensed, ready to fly the second he was released.

The presence withdrew. Greycub, still under an imposed silence, scuttled round as he sensed it moving around the house. A small noise, a scratch, then a crash as something fell to the floor and he knew it was inside the house and coming close to him - not this time towards a solid wall but to the sliding door, the door that could be opened. Greycub's lip curled back; he seemed to be able to follow the creature as it moved through the rooms of the house towards his little cell. The presence found the passageway along which his room lay. It came along and drew near. It stood outside the door. The door slid open.

The air was suddenly full of that wonderful, mysterious scent that was himself and at the same time so much more. Greycub flattened himself on the ground, licking his lips but keeping his silence, eager and terrified. A great beast came into the kennel. It licked its pale jaws. The light shone thin upon its silver flanks and front. It came at him, pushed him over onto his back, sniffed him, and began to lick.

Silver's long wolf's tongue licked away the layers of

scent that wrapped him up in a fog - licked away the smell of blankets, the smell of little Jenny, the reek of the Hunter's hand; licked away dog food and wet plastic bowls, the pungent reek of disinfectant and soap. She licked away the confusing layers of kennels, of the foster-mother dog and her pups, the smell of deerhounds and kennel maids, of the Breeder and his soapy hands, of wet tiles and floorboards and dry biscuits. She licked away all the things of captivity, all the clustered rubbish that concealed him from himself, even the most distant human things - the smell of the boot of the Hunter's car, of his pocket, the smell of frozen wolf flesh in the deep freeze, where the victims were stored - all this she licked and licked away and at last all that was left was the pure wolf.

Greycub stopped trembling and relaxed under his mother's jaws. As she licked she cried wolf noises to him, noises he instantly knew, and that placed him clearly, not as a strange dog or a bad pet, but as wolf. He replied and she understood. When that exchange was over, Greycub knew what he was and who he was and the danger he was in.

Silver turned and he followed quietly and obediently, along the passage, through the lounge and across the living room, out of the window into the good world. He had come home.

Silver led her cub north-west. She knew very well what great danger she had put them all in by this desperate rescue. She could not count on the rain to hide their tracks this time. It was a clear, mild night - just the sort of night that would hold clues of scent in the earth. Tracks tonight would be easy to follow.

After she and Conna had made their way down south back to the house where they knew the Hunter lived, she had quickly discovered where Greycub was and wasted no time in recovering him. She had not known he was in no immediate danger. Had she known that, she would perhaps not have chosen so reckless a method of rescuing him as luring the Hunter away with those howls.

It was Conna's howls that had led the Hunter away. Now he was heading north-east, hoping to reach the river Ouse and shake the Hunter off, before looping round and reuniting with Silver in the woodland around Haslemere. Hopefully this would leave Silver and the inexperienced Greycub in safety, for the time being at least.

Silver had hesitated a long time before giving this difficult task to Conna. None of the wolves had ever managed to shake off the Hunter, except by luck. What chance had Conna on this night, when even the damp, warm earth and still weather were against him? Luck, great good luck was needed if he was to survive. In her heart, Silver doubted whether he would. At least he could run fast. The only alternative was for Silver to go herself but this would mean allowing the rescue itself to be taken out of her control, and this she would not do.

Silver knew that if the Hunter did manage to catch up with and kill Conna, he would then return to his house and pick up their tracks. For this reason she did her best to make their trail as confusing as possible. She had plenty of time - they had a few days' grace at least - and she concentrated on turning her scent into a maze. She walked along stream beds, swam up and down the little rivers of the chalk country, set down false tracks, doubled back - all the tricks of her wolf cunning.

This journey to Haslemere served as Greycub's education. He learned all the scents of the hedgerows and meadows, the tricks of hunting and tracking, as well as those of laying false and confusing trails. His mother, who had been a pack leader, made sure her son was equipped for his dangerous life. Greycub had no difficulty learning. This was knowledge that he was waiting for. His joy at discovering that his loneliness and strangeness in the kennels and with poor Jenny were all due to a craving for his real life now helped him to learn the true, quiet, wolfish way of stalking and walking unseen through the man-made countryside.

As Silver and Greycub made their way, the Hunter had already found Conna's tracks. At first he thought he was having great good luck that the wolf should howl so incautiously near his house; he thought his luck was even better when he found Tulley's Wood covered with prints. Jenny picked up the scent in a second, but even without her he could have followed the marks the wolf had made as he headed away up a footpath. But it was not long before the Hunter asked himself why the wolf had behaved like this. So many marks so easily seen, and this clear track - it was not like the wolves to give themselves away so easily.

The Hunter was in no hurry. He knew there were two wolves left and here were the tracks of just one. He decided, since he was near, that it would be a good thing to go back to the house before he began the hunt.

Silver had been more careful than Conna, but she had left traces, and, of course, Jenny picked up her scent in a moment. The Hunter found the open window, the ashtray broken on the floor. He found the single tracks leading up to the house and the double ones leading away. He decided that here was the better game. He began his hunt - not after Conna, as the wolves expected, but after Silver and Greycub.

As they neared the woods around Haslemere, Silver began to slow down. This was the centre of her old running ground, the hub of the great loop her pack of eleven wolves had travelled in the course of their hunting. As such it was an old meeting place. Now it was marked with danger. The Hunter had struck them there before; her own father had been murdered here. But it was not fear of the Hunter that slowed Silver down. She did not expect him yet. She knew Conna would not even try to lose him for three or four days, and it would certainly take him at least that long to catch her mate. It was fear for Conna that slowed her down. In her heart Silver was sure he did not have the skill to shake the implacable Hunter off his track. She was sure that the meeting place, when she arrived there, would be empty. It was that knowledge, that she was alone with her cub, that she lingered to avoid.

The ambush took her completely by surprise - but it was not the Hunter who caught them but Conna himself. Jumping hard out of a bush he bowled her right over and she yelped in surprise and fright. Then the two wolves rolled over and over, biting and licking and fighting a soft fight, full of love. Greycub, who did not know this even taller great beast, rushed in to protect his mother. But the newcomer just grabbed him in his jaws and tossed him up at the sky. By the time he was caught by Silver and rolled in a ball over and over he knew he was in no danger. For a brief minute the two wolves, joyful at seeing each other, relaxed all their rules and huffed and growled and yapped, kicking up the wet earth and the dead leaves on the ground. Then they got down to the serious introductions and welcomings - Silver on one side, Conna on the other, licking each other's mouths and lips, with little Greycub standing in the middle on his hind legs, trying to join in.

The first bolt took Conna directly through the neck. His spine was not severed, but the central artery to his head was cut, and he was able to crawl a few metres into the undergrowth before choking on his own blood. Silver jumped up in surprise and so the bolt intended for her head caught her instead on her chest, just above the shoulder. She did not cry out, but continued the jump in a run, leaping over the dying Conna into the shielding bushes all around. Greycub leapt after her as a third bolt struck the empty ground where he had stood. Behind a man's voice cursed.

The Hunter had been in range for two days. He had only been waiting for Conna to join them, to get the chance of killing all three together.

Chapter 9

Silver's wound was not so serious as last time but she needed time to rest and recover - time which she did not have. The initial run she made with Greycub took them a mile further north. There she lay down to gather breath. Greycub whined and licked her wound, but there was no time for sympathy. After only a few minutes, Silver picked herself up and forced herself on. Again she was on three legs. The other, though un-damaged, put an unbearable pressure on her shattered ribs.

In this last run Silver gave up any hope of throwing the Hunter off her scent; everything she had done had failed - all her tricks, all her cunning, all the centuries of wolf culture were useless before this man who had wiped out her race. There was little point laying false trails that fooled no one. Instead, she just ran, fast and straight, hoping that some chance would free her again from his attention. Rain, perhaps - but the sky above her was clear and blue, the air still. Only a few thin white clouds scattered at the edges of the afternoon.

Behind, the Hunter understood her intention and he too pushed on as fast as he was able. Poor Jenny, miserable to her core, kept looking up at him and trying to lick his hand, unable to understand. He gave her no reassurance but cursed her on. He was keen to end his three-year hunt. He did not even bother to take care of Conna's corpse but buried him in a sack, hoping to be back soon enough to deal with him before the skin was much damaged by decay.

Silver continued north-west. She avoided villages, except in the dead of night. She followed the beds of streams from time to time, but beyond this she wasted no time with cunning, but ran and ran. She cut through woodland along a stream in a valley north-west of the village of Liphook and then turned north to avoid Alton. When she hit the river Wey she swam upstream a couple of miles, and then directly north, curving a little to avoid Farnham. All the time she was losing blood and getting weaker. They did not stop to eat; they drank as they swam. There was no plan, only to go as far as they could and then to hide, and to hope.

The wolves ran into the Basingstoke canal at Crookham Village. For the last time they took to the water and swam westwards. Silver, with a pale pink wake leaking behind her, was now at the very end of her strength. Greycub swam forward and back, forward and back, trying to bring her along. But now it was obvious she was finished. The cold water, that had refreshed her momentarily when they plunged in, drained away the last of her strength. With difficulty she clambered out and staggered along the banks, heading north. Soon they came to a motorway and here Silver did not pause but cut straight across, putting one last barrier between her and her pursuer. Briefly, horns blared, brakes squeaked as the two last wolves crawled across six lanes and up the bank on the other side. They walked along, seeking a place to make their last stand.

A cluster of old farm buildings, tumbledown and with the roof half off, overlooked the motorway, unused ever since the road had been built. Silver chose a stall close to the door of one of these buildings. There was just one way in; the only window was blocked by a stack of heavy timbers leaning up against it. It was dark. From outside you could not see in, and the Hunter would certainly have to enter before he could see well enough to shoot.

Cornered with her last pup, her whole pack and race wiped out, only now did Silver consider attacking the man. He would have to enter to kill her. She would see him before he saw her. She was weak, wounded and he was armed and strong. But there was at least a chance she could take him. Once she got in close he would be unable to use his bow and then, armed with her teeth and claws, the advantage would be hers. Silver settled herself down to one side of the entrance, well hidden from anyone outside. Greycub settled down next to her, licking again at her wound, and whining fearfully. For a few hours, the two wolves snatched some sleep.

Later Greycub went to try and hunt. After a whole hour he came back proudly with a single scrawny old rat, which poor Silver, forgetting herself, swallowed in one bite. Somewhat surprised that his great work should be dealt with so quickly - it was his first kill - Greycub looked so put out that his mother huffed at him, which is a wolf's laugh. Then she repented as she realised that he had eaten nothing for two days, and thanked him by licking his face. Greycub had to go out after more rats or go hungry. Four hours brought two more, which they shared, and by then he was too tired to hunt. Curling up in his mother's belly, his nose tucked under her tail, Greycub went to sleep.

Silver lay awake, her ears cocked to the front of the stall, and waited.

A day later the Hunter arrived.

She knew instantly. He made no noise, but she caught

the smell of him and his dog. Immediately she took Greycub between her paws, and tensed herself, ready to launch herself the second he came within reach. It was unheard of for a wolf to attack a human being, but this man had lost his right to live. She prepared to kill.

The Hunter was in no hurry now that he had his prey cornered. He knew very well that she would not leave Greycub, and that he had all the time in the world to plot his kill, to make absolutely sure it worked the way he wanted it to. Now that the wolves were only metres away, poor little Jenny was in fits, flattening herself on the ground, begging and pleading but obedient. He tied her up away from the entrance and swore her to silence, while he checked the lie of the land.

He noted the big timbers leaning up against the side that blocked off the only other exit, and peered in among them. The heavy beams were crammed up right against the window, leaving only a narrow space - there was no way she could sneak out the back.

The Hunter came back and sat on the ground next to Jenny to think. She licked his hand and gazed at him, but he pushed her thoughtlessly away as he plotted the kill. He did not dare go straight in the front way. It is not wise to come up upon a wounded mother, cornered with her pup, and he did not want to endanger himself.

Leaving Jenny at the front, and staying well back so the wolf did not know he was moving, the Hunter crept round behind, back to the window. He took from inside his coat a small hand gun. Just below the embankment, the motorway traffic roared past, thick and furious. Normally he would not dare use a gun, because of the noise it made, but here no one would hear anything.

Holding the gun at arm's length before him the Hunter began to squeeze his way in among the timbers, sliding his body, breathing in, squashing himself silently up until, through narrow cracks, he could see inside.

Now the wolf, instead of being in the dark was palely silhouetted in the light coming in the front of the stall. The Hunter could see her ears pricked, pointing forward, her eyes fixed on the point where Jenny was hidden. He saw her shift on her haunches, saw how tense she was and he knew she had his death on her mind. It gave him a cold feeling to think that after so many years he had become the prey. But it was clear the wolf did not know where he was; he had the advantage.

The Hunter pushed still closer, holding the gun before him like the head of a snake nearer and silently nearer to the cracks in the window. He was wedged so tightly he had to breathe out, push himself deeper, breathe in, breathe again and push, snaking his way into the wood pile, taking his air in small sips, moving slowly, slowly, making no noise - until at last he was able to hold his gun at the edge of the hidden window. He meant to shoot the wolf in the back of her head.

Down below on the carriageway a convoy of heavy lorries thundered past. The ground shivered under him and the surrounding timbers rattled slightly. The wolf still focused straight ahead. The Hunter had to stand on tiptoe so he could see the part of the wolf's head he wanted. He took aim, and fired.

The shot echoed and shuddered all around the stall and cracked in his ears. He had to blink and when he looked up he thought for a second he had missed, for the wolf was almost in the same position. But now her head was down, fallen onto her paws, and her ears relaxed. Blood began to gather in the hair around her neck. The cub silently nosed his mother's dead head, before casting a furious look into the crevice where the predator hid. Then he fled out of the building. The Hunter turned his gun on him but the crack was too small, the metal barrel clicked uselessly on the wood.

The Hunter began to squeeze backwards as fast as he could out of the crevice. He could not move his gun hand or even turn his head, and he had to feel his way with his feet. Then, to his horror there was a noise and a low growl - behind him. He was so surprised he let out a thin scream and tried to turn round, but he was still wedged in too tightly. He was trapped and blind. A feeling of panic surged through him. He wanted to pant but was squeezed so tight he was unable to do even that. The only thing to do was to back further out towards the noise. He squeezed back little by little and at last he was able to turn his head and see what beast had come upon him, helpless, his gun trapped on the other side of his body.

It was Greycub. He was standing in the opening, his teeth bared, growling at the killer.

The Hunter laughed with relief. The cub was far too small to do him any harm.

'You - you're next,' he told the cub. 'You're the last one.' The cub did not move at his voice. The Hunter frowned. It was as if the young beast knew his gun was trapped behind him and he could not fire. This annoyed the Hunter, and he tried to scare Greycub off.

'Hah!' he shouted suddenly. The cub jumped but to his surprise did not run. Instead, he growled louder and then jumped up and caught the Hunter with his teeth in the soft flesh on the side of his leg and tugged as hard as he could.

'Hi - get off, get off.' The Hunter kicked and screamed, but the young wolf only bit deeper and growled louder.

'Jenny - damn you, come here!' the Hunter screamed; but the terrier was still tied up in front of the building, and all she could do was bark furiously. The Hunter tried to force his way out and free his hand but his own panting breath was wedging him more firmly in. The blood flowed and the cub bit again. The Hunter had to shuffle forward against those tiny sharp teeth - it felt as if there were a thousand of them - and at last he found a widening in the passage and swung his hand round. Instantly Greycub let go and ran off round the corner and out of sight. The Hunter dropped to his knee and clutched his wound.

'Little swine. I'll kill you . . . ' he growled. Jenny was barking madly round the other side of the stall. 'What good's barking, you idiot?' he yelled. He bent round to try and see the wound.

It was not deep, though Greycub had done all the damage he could. But it was still the worst wound that the Hunter had ever suffered from an animal, and he swore Greycub would not escape.

The wolfcub clambered down the slope of the cutting onto the motorway and turned east, just because he and Silver had been travelling west when they had been ambushed. Sticking to the hard shoulder, and ignoring the cars hurtling past at such violent speeds, he ran hard for the first few miles. The he settled down to a steady trot, not so fast as to wear himself out, but as fast as he

71

could bear. He did not think he could escape. If a great creature like Silver was unable to shake the Hunter off, how could an animal like himself even dream of it? He kept up his steady run, mile after mile. It did seem to him that the stink of all the cars zooming past might help to disguise his scent. He did not know or understand that it was Jenny rather than the Hunter who followed him, and he was not old enough or wise enough to work out that on the hard shoulder, where few cars drove, his scent would be untouched.

The Hunter wasted no time on the older wolf before he began his hunt for the cub. He was keen to kill again. His leg, still sore from Greycub's attack, reminded him that he owed this particular wolf a lesson. And of course, this was the very last wolf in all England. This was the one he wanted above all.

He walked quickly, nervous lest this most important prey of all might get killed on the big road. He quickly found the point where Greycub had moved off the grass and onto the tarmac and the hard shoulder of the M3.

Now the Hunter had a problem. It was illegal to walk on the motorway. On his own he might pretend his car had broken down, but with a dog, the first police car that passed would surely stop him. The Hunter marked down where the cub had joined the road and then left the scene and made his way back to his home as fast as he could to return the next evening with his own car. He left it on the hard shoulder below the scene of the killing. Now, he could pretend he had broken down, and no one would see Jenny in the dark.

He had no doubt he would catch and kill the wolfcub. Greycub was so young, he knew so little. Of course, the

Hunter could see nothing on the hard tarmac and had to rely on Jenny's sharp nose, but Jenny had never let him down yet. Tonight she was over-excited. It had been a mistake letting her mother that cub. It never occurred to the Hunter for even a second that his dog would betray him and lead him astray from the scent. He was her master. He had trained her, he believed absolutely in her. She would jump to her death at his command because she was his.

He began to walk up the road in the direction the tracks had led encouraging Jenny to pick up the scent. She wagged her tail and sniffed and snuffled up and down the grass by the side of the tarmac. For a second it seemed that she had the scent. But then she stopped and fawned, wagged her tail, whined.

'Get on with it!' he cried. She whined again and ran up and down the grass by the hard shoulder. She seemed unable to go further.

Perhaps the roar of the traffic was frightening her, he thought, or else the stink of all those passing cars had drowned the wolfcub's scent. That must be it; the cub had run on the carriageway itself, and passing cars had drowned the scent. It occurred to him that maybe those same cars had killed the cub. All he could do was walk along until Jenny found the point where Greycub left the road - if he ever had.

After four miles in one direction the Hunter decided the cub must have gone the other way. He walked back and began again in the opposite direction. After another four miles he wondered if the cub hadn't crossed to the other side, and began to worry that a car might get Greycub before he did. He crossed the motorway at the next bridge and returned to try on the other side.

Jenny found nothing. She grinned madly and jumped up and down, fawned and cried.

'What's wrong, girl?' The Hunter frowned. 'We'll get him - don't worry,' he said. He did not want her anxiety at failure to get in the way of her skills.

The next night the Hunter returned and covered ten miles on either side of the point where the tracks had gone onto the road, but still he found nothing. The next day he tried walking thirty miles up the road in the direction the tracks had gone in when they went onto the road. By the time he had covered that distance on each side of the road in both directions, he knew he had lost.

The cub must have been hit by a car. Bitterly he realised that he had missed his chance to kill this last of its kind. The ignorant driver who must have heaped the cub into his boot probably thought he had hit a stray mongrel. There was no other explanation.

The hunt was over.

Chapter 10

Greycub ran up the motorway for three miles. Then some instinct made him turn south.

It was instinct perhaps that told him that his home, the place where his ancestors had lived for generations, was to the south - that sent his flat, wide puppy-paws flapping and padding up and down for hours along roads, over fields, padding away, to find his way back. It was instinct that told him he was still too young to survive on his own. He did not even try to find food. He stopped at puddles and streams to drink. And all the time, south, south. He crossed rivers and roads, nearly causing an accident more than once. He ran blindly and directly, without a pause. He was running for his life.

It could not have been just instinct that led him to one particular corner of Surrey. Greycub had no knowledge of where he was heading, although he knew he had a goal. He had no memory of his very early life, before the Breeder, but somehow he had fixed in him a sense of home, of safety. It was a place Silver could never have turned to. She had grown up in the wild and for her all humans were enemies. In the end, that failure to adapt had cost her her life. But Greycub, who had lived with people, had no such inhibitions.

Long after his paws were raw and bleeding, he continued to run. On the morning of the third day he padded almost blind with fatigue along the small road that led to High Pond Farm and through a gate that he could not remember, right up into the farmyard. Then, he sat down and waited.

Unfortunately for Greycub there was no one there at the time. Ben was up in his room doing his homework and both his mother and father were out. It was not until John Tilley came back an hour later on the tractor that he saw a strange little dog sitting in the middle of the yard. He thought how odd it was that it did not move. It just turned his head to look at him, rather shakily. The poor little thing seemed dead beat. He got off the tractor and went down to have a closer look. Then he noticed the smoky blue eyes, only just beginning to turn amber. It was not until he had it in his hands that he remembered the strange grey silver and pale gold coat, and saw that the pup was just exactly the right age.

'It's that damn cub come back - he's found his way - Ben!' he shouted and ran to the house with his find.

Chapter 11

Greycub's marathon - it was an astounding journey for such a small cub, with no food and no rest - had won him his safety, but he was in a trauma of shock, exhaustion and hunger when John Tilley found him in the farmyard. After a meal of minced meat in warm milk he fell straight to sleep and carried on sleeping for the whole day and the following night. He did not even wake up when Mr Tilley dressed his raw paws with antiseptic. He jerked a little in his sleep as the stinging liquid was dabbed on and he cried, but never woke up.

He spent the night in Ben's room. He was not allowed in the bed as Mrs Tilley was worried he would wet it, or worse, and Ben had to promise to keep him in a basket on the floor. As soon as his parents had said goodnight he lifted the sleeping wolfcub out and snuggled him in the warm next to him.

'If you wet, I'll say I did it,' he whispered. Greycub licked his lips in his sleep and began to snore.

While Greycub recovered his strength, the Tilleys waited anxiously for the Hunter to return. All who knew of the wolves had been on the alert for the killer ever since he had attacked the Tilleys' barn, but there had been no sign of either him or the wolves. Greycub was the first wolf anyone had seen for months and now the neighbourhood was re-alerted. Every strange face was closely scrutinised, every car that parked in the back ways examined and noted. But the Hunter believed Greycub dead and it never occurred to him that the cub could possibly have gone that far, or could know where the farm was. The Tilleys also hoped to see Silver and Conna again. They almost forced themselves to believe that there were wolves out there somewhere, even though none ever again crossed the fields or left their tracks on the bridleway at night. Greycub, too, waited and hoped. Once again, he was separated from his kind.

For the first fortnight after his return he stayed indoors, refused to go out and jumped at the slightest noise. Mr Tilley's voice frightened him badly, because it reminded him of the voice of the man who had come upon him and slaughtered his family. But gradually he calmed down and in the evenings, as he had done in the Hunter's house, he sat outside and sang. Perhaps he expected Silver to come back. Perhaps it was the hope, the belief that another great and wonderful creature would appear once more and take him back to his own kind. Of course, no such beast came; there were none left to rescue him.

After a time the Tilleys began to wonder what to do with their wild guest. Even Ben, who loved the wolf, knew that such an animal was not so much a member of their household as a kind of visitor they were privileged to have, and who would one day leave. His parents were frightened that as he grew up the age-old fear of humankind would come back and turn Greycub savage. By the time he was six months old he was no longer a cub, but a lean young wolf. As yet, there was no sign of fear or anger in him.

The Tilleys tried to pass Greycub off as a dog among visitors to the farm, but it was clear to anyone that this was a very strange kind of dog indeed. Had Greycub known this he would have been most offended. He looked down on all dogs, although they did their best to be friends with him. Clearly he regarded them as very inferior creatures, lacking in grace, manners and intelligence and with no pride whatsoever.

If Ben ever thought that a wolf was similar to a dog, he soon realised how crude that idea was. The farm dogs, for instance, once they realised that a person was a friend of the family, would let the stranger take all sorts of liberties. They would roll on their bellies and gurgle and beg for scraps and creep away with their tail between their legs when told, 'No!'

Not Greycub. Anyone who tried to pat him on the head or ruffle his ears was shaken off with a quick jerk of the head, although he never snapped - that would be bad manners. He just stalked out of the room full of dignity, or sat down at a good distance with a look that clearly said, 'Do you mind?' Even Ben could not take such liberties. And yet it was not that Greycub did not love him. Whenever Ben was upset or hurt, suddenly Greycub's nose would be in the palm of his hand. And whenever Ben needed him or wanted him he always seemed to know.

Perhaps the main difference betweend Greycub and a dog was his pride and his intelligence. This came out very strongly when Mr Tilley tried to make him wear a collar. Mr Tilley thought that since he would one day grow into a very large and possibly dangerous animal, he ought to get used to wearing a collar and a lead and to being tethered. Greycub disagreed.

Once, and once only, Mr Tilley took him by surprise by slipping on the collar while he was eating, and Greycub spent the rest of the day wandering about trying to peer down his nose to see what unpleasantness was on his neck. Then Mr Tilley clipped a chain onto the collar, and slipped the other end of the chain, a steel loop, over a stake in the yard.

Greycub tested the chain with his teeth, rattled it a bit, looked at Mr Tilley, then at Ben, who shrugged sympathetically. Then he retired in disgust and sat with his back to Mr Tilley, who dusted his hands at a job well done, and went into the kitchen for a cup of tea.

This stake and chain had been used by Mr Tilley for his own dogs for years and he never doubted for a second that Greycub would do what all the others had done, and lie down to wait for his release at Mr Tilley's convenience. A few minutes later, however, sitting with his tea at the kitchen table, he happened to glance out of the window and was treated to the sight of Greycub on his hind legs, easing the steel ring, held firmly between his teeth, over the top of the stake.

'Hoy!' shouted Mr Tilley - too late. Just as he ran out of the house, Greycub ran out of the yard, the chain rattling behind him. When he came back later that night, neither collar nor chain was to be seen, and Mr Tilley never saw them again for five years, when he found both, very well rusted by now, at the bottom of a pond three miles away from the farmhouse.

After that the mere sight of a collar or the rattle of a chain sent Greycub hurtling off as fast as his legs could go. Mr Tilley made dark noises about obedience and 'problems later on . . . ' but for the time being, Greycub wore no collar and no chain.

About the same time, Greycub seemed to stop noticing that Mr Tilley existed at all. Evidently that sort of behaviour put him beneath contempt, on a level slightly below the farm dogs, a kind of cat or a goat with no manners, who happened to walk on two legs.

Things remained like this for some time, in a stalemate, but it couldn't stay that way for long. Mr Tilley kept muttering threats about 'taking that damn animal in hand'. In the end he got the excuse he needed when Greycub fell out badly with Mrs Tilley.

For some time a big pile of cushions on the living room floor had been Greycub's bed, and every evening after dinner he rested on this before going out on his own for a run. Soon however, he began to take less and less food from the Tilleys, preferring to catch his own in the farm fields and outhouses. He ate a lot of mice, which pleased Mr Tilley, and some rabbits, which was a good thing too. The problem arose when he started to bring them home to finish off. Mrs Tilley noticed this one evening when watching television. She happened to look up and there was Greycub chewing a rabbit's head on the cushions.

'You beast!' she cried, jumping up and snatching it from him before hurling it dramatically out of the window.

Greycub was most offended. He looked at her in surprise as if to say, 'How would you like it if I snatched your dinner off you in such a rude, unpleasant way?' Mrs Tilley did not take the point, however, and from that night on, Greycub insisted on bringing his rabbits home and eating them on the cushions. It was a matter of pride with him. It was equally a matter of pride with Mrs Tilley. She now removed the cushions. Greycub ate the rabbits' heads on the sofa. She locked him out. He waited until next morning to eat his dinner.

This could not go on, it was costing a fortune in cleaning bills. Whatever else you could say about

Greycub's manners, he certainly knew how to spread his dinner around.

Mr Tilley, who fancied himself as something of an expert with dog training, pounced on the occasion. It was time to take Greycub 'in hand'.

Mr Tilley favoured the firm but kind approach. He considered it necessary that the trainee dog should know who was master, and respect the master's wishes. The dog should not be so much afraid of his master, as in awe of him. A good dog, Mr Tilley considered, regarded it as his aim in life to please the master, and would be deeply ashamed, humiliated in fact, at the idea of so far letting him down as to displease him. For the purposes of the training, Mr Tilley was to be master.

They began with the simple business of 'coming when called'.

The basic trouble with this was that Greycub took not the slightest notice. Mr Tilley tried walking off a few metres and then calling the cub, holding out a piece of biscuit in his hand. Greycub checked with Ben; but Ben had been told to keep quiet, and without any encouraging noises from him, Greycub just sat, regarding the biscuit gravely, and Mr Tilley not at all. After several minutes of encouragingly calling, 'Come on, boy - here, come on!' and whistling bravely, Mr Tilley stood up.

'He's not very hungry perhaps,' he muttered.

'Go and get it, go on, Greycub,' said Ben, and Greycub promptly trotted over, took the biscuit and trotted back to Ben's side.

'Must be one of those one-man dogs you hear about,' growled Mr Tilley.

It was much easier getting Greycub to come when Ben called. The difficulty was getting him to wait while Ben walked away. In fact, Mr Tilley had to hold him by the fur on the back of his head - he still wore no collar - and Greycub tended to run to Ben not when he was called, but when he was let go, which indicated it was nothing to do with the call at all.

Mr Tilley found all this very discouraging. 'He's got to be properly trained, there's no two ways about it,' he said darkly.

'It isn't as though he's bad,' pointed out Ben. This in general was true. Greycub respected other people's space and needs. Only in the matter of his own space was he particular, such as the wearing of collars and whether or not he was allowed to eat his own dinner on his own bed.

This carried no weight with Mr Tilley, who pointed out that *he* wasn't allowed to get his dinner all over his bed, so why should Greycub?

They spent the rest of the afternoon teaching the wolf to walk to heel. This was easy. Ben walked along and Greycub followed him. He didn't even need a lead. It was not so easy when Mr Tilley's were the heels involved, however. Greycub tended to wander off to one side or the other. He did not really seem to appear to be aware that they were going anywhere in particular and suddenly discovered that there were a great many things, like daisies and dandelions or even fairly boring patches of grass, that were a great deal more interesting than Mr Tilley's heels. Of course, with a lead, it was different. Mr Tilley could drag him along behind easily enough, but this, as he rather petulantly pointed out, was not the point.

'He's supposed to follow me,' he complained.

They had similar trouble with fetching the stick and

giving it back. Greycub didn't mind giving the stick back. The thing was you had to give it to him first and then take it off him before he dropped it. As for chasing after it, he didn't see the point. Mr Tilley got quite exhausted going to and fro with that stick. Even Ben couldn't make Greycub see what he was supposed to do. He just sat there wagging his tail excitedly, while Mr Tilley danced about waving the stick in the air. When he threw it, they all watched it sail away through the air, and then Greycub turned back to see what this amusing man would do next.

Mr Tilley, chastened by the experience, decided not to humiliate himself further, and they went home. There was no more talk of training.

There was still the matter of the rabbits' heads to be sorted out. It was clear to Ben, if not to Greycub, that his mother was going to be a harder nut to crack than his father. Those heads were making quite a mess.

Mrs Tilley decided to try and ignore it, and hoped that would satisfy honour. It did not. Greycub continued to eat the heads and began to growl rather louder than necessary when he chewed them, as if to drive the point home. Mrs Tilley looked straight ahead and only twitched slightly. But at last she broke.

'I can't stand it!' she shouted. 'I won't - my covers - the whole place stinks and it's filthy!' And she rushed out of the room very upset.

Greycub looked mildly about him as if unaware of what the fuss was about. Mr Tilley looked dark. Ben went to sit by Greycub. He did not know what to do. In the kitchen his mother bashed about, doing the washing-up or something.

'Oh, Greycub,' he said. 'You can't keep doing it.

Won't you please just eat them outside?'

Greycub got up, picked up the rabbit's head and walked into the kitchen. He scratched at the back door, which Mrs Tilley opened, and then dropped the head into the rubbish before coming back and lying quietly, with only a trace of smugness, on his cushions, while Mrs Tilley watched open-jawed from the kitchen doorway.

No one would say that Greycub knew exactly what the world 'please' meant, but something in Ben's tone indicated to him that he was not being told but being asked. And that made the difference. Ben soon found that if you wanted Greycub to do anything, you had to ask him nicely.

Greycub grew up fast. He reached his full height at the end of a year and began to put on muscle rapidly. He was a big wolf, taller than either his mother or father and his coat was a shimmering field of silver flecked with gold. He was a handsome animal by any standards and Ben soon grew tired of fending off questions about his breed.

As he grew, his wolfish nature became stronger. He would have less and less to do with dogs and was becoming short-tempered in dealing with them. He showed no signs of temper with Ben but soon, to Mr and Mrs Tilley's alarm, he began to show his temper with them and any other people, especially when Ben was not around. About the same time Greycub took to leaving the farm on journeys of his own, at first just for a few hours, but then for whole days at a time. Mr Tilley worried about the sheep, Ben worried about the roads; but Silver had taught Greycub well and he knew enough to avoid all of these.

One night, sixteen months after Greycub had turned up at the farm, Ben took him out for a run up the bridleway before going to bed. He stood and watched as the animal roamed up and down sniffing. It was sad how often Greycub paused and waited with his ears cocked at some noise at the end of the garden. Ben guessed what he was listening for, and wondered for the hundredth time if he would ever hear it. Now, Greycub whined and came back to Ben. He rubbed the back of his head against the boy's legs and ran a little way up the road. There he stood, with his back to him, looking at him over his shoulder, crying a little.

'What is it, boy?' asked Ben. He called Greycub to him, but for the first time the wolf did not obey. He turned and sat watching his friend with a curious expression.

Ben had an empty feeling in his stomach.

'What's wrong, Grey?' he asked. Greycub thumped his tail and shook himself. He walked up to Ben and again rubbed his head on his leg, before walking off again and sitting.

'Come inside, Greycub,' said Ben. Neither of them moved. He walked up to him and held his great head in his arms.

'You're going to go, aren't you?' he said. Greycub whined and pawed at his jacket, and licked at Ben's wet face.

'You wouldn't lick me if you knew what I'd done,' said Ben in a choked voice.

In a minute Ben went on, 'I know you're not really mine. You were just waiting here. But I did want you to stay.'

Greycub stood on his hind legs with his paws on Ben's shoulders and licked his face. If he could he would have told Ben that there was no other family, no other person for him - just the longing for his own kind that was taking him away. But of course he could say none of this. He jumped back down. Ben rubbed his ears and said goodbye. Greycub huffed, licked his hand once and ran lightly up the bridleway for a few metres, before he cut off through the hedge and disappeared. Ben never saw him again.

Chapter 12

Greycub did not stay in Surrey, although he knew that this was his ancestral home. Perhaps Silver had communicated to him that the wolves had left that area. Instead he went north, cutting directly through London on his way. He travelled at night, keeping to the small roads except very late when there was no traffic. A taxi driver, who had just dropped off a fare near Crystal Palace saw him jump over the park fence, and thought to himself that people who wanted a big dog like that should look after it properly. A man with no home saw him in a little street east of the Elephant and Castle and called him over to share some bread, but Greycub ignored him, too. He crossed the river at Westminster Bridge at three in the morning, and was beyond Swiss Cottage by dawn. He slept under the foundations of an old house that day. The next night he was clear of the city and began searching seriously with his nose.

Of Greycub's search there is not enough time to tell here. It carried him right round the country, up to Scotland, where he lingered, liking the wilderness. He even investigated some of the islands off the west coast, swimming out to see if any wolves still lived on those remote places, but of course finding none. He came back down across the border after eighteen months and headed into Cumbria. Then he went through the English and Welsh counties one by one.

Of course he found wolves in the zoos, and sniffed these foreign animals through the bars. Possibly he would have settled with them had he been able to get in, but that was no more possible than it was for them to get out and anyway, the breed of English wolves with their pale silver and blond coats, had been separated for so long from the continental wolves that they were really a different breed, and he wanted his own. He hung around them for a few nights, and then continued his search.

It took two years before Greycub realised that there truly were no more wolves. He went down to Sussex last of all. He found the house on the Downs were he had been weaned - and that other house where the Hunter kept him. But the Hunter had gone. A few months had been enough to convince him there were no more wolves to be had. He believed Greycub had died on the M3 that night, and his body removed. He had only taken his house on the Downs to be among his prey, and now he had no more prey he moved on. Greycub passed down into the very garden where he had taken his runs with Jenny; but that was long ago and the scents were long washed away. He sniffed around the garden, found as usual nothing, and continued away up the lanes on his fruitless hunt.

One of the last places Greycub visited before he gave up was High Pond Farm. He walked down the bridle-way, sniffing old familiar smells of Ben and Mr and Mrs Tilley. This was a place of good memories. When he came to the farm itself, Greycub stopped outside the yard and sniffed the air. He had avoided humans completely in the past two years. Now, because he knew these were friendly, he paused. But Greycub was a wild wolf now, no longer a cub. Those two years had made it impossible for him to live in a house and he was unable to bear a human hand on his head. The dogs barked;

Greycub snorted and ran off into a field that once held cabbages. Now it was planted with a bright yellow crop of rape. The wolf ran low across the ground that no longer held the marks of his kind, shaking the pollen until he emerged, yellow-dusted, on the other side into the woodland where, unknown to him, his pack had been finally destroyed.

For a further year Greycub wandered up and down the country, always moving on, always alone. As time passed he became more and more wary of people, more and more he wanted not even to smell them. So at last he wandered up into the wilderness of Scotland, the only place in the British Isles where he could feel truly remote from human kind. There he made his home.

Greycub established a territory, a great loop in the central mountains. He lived off game and became used to his own company. As a naturally sociable animal it was a wretched life for a wolf. Greycub, who had never known that close, warm family life except for the company of his mother for a few short days, grew into a hard, aloof animal. He was a relic, in whom wolf culture had never blossomed. The society that had given his kind a way of life for so long was already extinct. He was a ghost, only outwardly a wild wolf. His narrow life had no hope of widening. He became shyer of men, more and more aloof from the other wildlife. He lost his adventurous spirit, and stuck to the same paths and routes every day, every week, and his life became a mere routine.

While inside his heart shrank, his body grew. Within a few years he reached his prime - a great burly wolf, his shoulders hard rolls of muscle, his long legs capable of covering miles at an easy trot.

Although Greycub had his own territory, he did not always stick to it. From time to time he wandered off, restlessly covering mile after mile, because he was tired of being alone and could not stay still any longer.

After two years in the Highlands, one such urge came over him and he found himself on the move again. This time he went west, out of the central hills, to the twisted rocks of the Scottish west coast. There he wandered north into country he had not been in for many years.

It was a frosty October day. Greycub was slowing down. He had the past day crossed human tracks four or five times and he was beginning to think of turning back and returning to his own land. He was sniffing for the scent of the small roe deer that lived on the edge of a fir plantation, when he came to a scent that stopped him in his tracks.

Greycub whined and scratched at the earth. He sniffed again and then sank to the ground, his legs taut under him. He looked around him. Then he stood up and sniffed the wind. The tip of his tail twitched with excitement.

Greycub had crossed a scent he had never expected to find again.

It was the scent of the Hunter.

Chapter 13

Once he had run out of wolves, the Hunter had travelled around the world: to Asia for tigers and the rare Indian lion, to Africa for white rhino, South America for jaguar. He had spent over a year in Java, hunting the very rare Javanese rhino, and when he got one moved on, around the world, seeking more trophies. Homeless for a number of years and living in hotels or camps wherever his passion for killing led him, he at last wanted to establish a base for himself and his macabre collection. He finally settled on a house on the remote west coast of Scotland, a converted barn from a long disused settlement close by the shaly sea coast. In this place, far from prying eyes, he now lived in between his journeys round the world.

Most of his collection was in trunks, packed away, since even in this remote place he did not dare openly display his illegal trophies. But in one large room, with a window overlooked by a steep bank, he did have on show the products of the hunt he held closest to his heart.

That autumn he had been living in the house, only vaguely planning his next expedition. He was growing tired of globe-trotting; it seemed to him he had killed everything worth killing and he was glad of the rest. Now, he had a visitor. An old friend of his had come to stay, another hunter. The two men had eaten a good meal and now they had moved into the large well-lit room with the big window. A fire was blazing, the armchairs were deep in soft pelts. The two men were drinking whisky. By the fire, half buried under a pile of wolf skins, lay a small, crooked white dog. Jenny was still with her master.

The room was full of dead wolves - their skins, their skulls, their teeth. There were wolves' skins eight deep on the sofa and draped over the chairs on which the men sat. There were skins heaped lavishly on the floor. There were a couple of wolves stuffed and mounted in one corner, with cubs sitting around their feet, and a wolf's skull snarled coldly and blindly from the mantelpiece. There were heads mounted on the wall, blind things, worse than dead, that no longer even smelled like wolf, gathering dust on their dry teeth and black gums. All the wolf skins in there shared one thing: they all had somewhere about them the pale blond fur that dusted Greycub's flanks. There were the remains of seventy-two wolves in that room, which was the number of the total English wolf pack when the Hunter found them.

Inside the fire crackled. The Hunter had central heating in the house but in this room it was never on. The dry heat would have been bad for the skins.

'I got that one in Hastings,' he was saying to his friend. 'He was a clever dog, that one! Never stayed far away from humans as soon as he knew I was on his trail. He knew I couldn't attract attention, you see. He lived out of dustbins for a month, never left people's gardens, but I tracked him down. I got him under Hastings pier in the end.'

The other man grunted and sipped his whisky. He was just back from a trip to Africa. He had stories of his own he wanted to boast to the Hunter about, but he had nothing to compete with this.

'Wolves in Sussex - it doesn't seem possible,' he murmured. 'I'd never have believed it from anyone else but you.'

'They didn't stay in Sussex long once they realised someone was onto them. That group there' - he pointed at a heap of skins over the back of the settee - 'they took up residence in South London. I guess they thought they'd be safe up there. But I found them.'

'Oh, come on,' said the other man. 'You don't try to tell me they knew you were onto them ...?'

'I promise you - each one was more difficult than the last. That Hastings dog was number twenty-four. Now that one' - he pointed up to an animal with a blond and grey face - 'number thirty-five. She was a devil. She climbed trees - would you believe that? A wolf up a tree. She got me that way a number of times. The trail just vanished. I couldn't work out what was going on. But then one day the jays found her and started kicking up a racket. I just looked up and there she was. We looked straight at one another, just a few metres away. She knew what was coming. I took my time. I walked round the side and got her in the ear so as not to spoil her skin. Beautiful, isn't she?'

'They're lovely animals. You must have killed dozens. Are they all English?'

'Every one an English wolf.'

'And how many are there left? Any idea?'

'None.'

'What? You killed them all?'

'Every single one.'

'Isn't that ...'

'What?'

'A bit of a pity, don't you think?'

The Hunter laughed. 'Jealous, that's what you are. You'll never have an English wolf hide on your wall - never. No one will, except me. Now, don't get all sentimental on me. How many animals have you killed in your life?'

'But I never wiped out a whole breed - are you sure there are none left?'

'I shot them all - all bar one, that is. The very last one, too. Now that was a pity - but it was only a cub, just a few weeks old. Got himself flattened on the M3. There's none left for you, I'm afraid. I had them all.'

Out in the cold night hidden in darkness, on the slope above the house, the last wolf lay hidden in the long grass, looking down into the room full of death. Greycub saw the skins and the heads, the stuffed animals - the stuffed cubs were his own sisters but they meant nothing to him. They were no longer wolves. Their wolf smell had gone from them, washed away with chemicals used to cure the skins. Their wolf spirit had been purged so completely that to Greycub they meant less than the merest live beetle he sniffed on his nightly wanderings. But he recognised Jenny - and one of the men below him. He whined slightly and shuffled on his belly. Then he turned and crept back out of the grass away from the garden falling away below him. He trotted quietly up the road, past the house. There were no signs of urgency or hurry in his manner.

Greycub followed rather less than his usual precautions, carelessly stepping off the road onto the grass verge occasionally, scratching the dirt with his paw and sniffing for food just to one side of his track. Soon he left the road and crossed a field, squeezing under a fence that lightly scratched his back, and then onto the rocky seashore. On this rocky northern coast he left no tracks at all, but further away from the sea there was some sand with tufts of marram grass, and here he left tracks. He found some mice living under an old heap of car tyres which he ate before heading off inland again.

Greycub made his way for several miles in this manner, always keeping close to the seashore, never going more than a mile inland. To all intents he was on a night-time foraging expedition, taking time to root about in areas of woodland, to investigate for fish and crabs in the shallow rock pools. After many miles he came to a place where the water had found a way past the shale ridges of the coast to form a long still lagoon. This water lay in a basin cut off from the body of the ocean by a long series of ridges, hiding the lagoon and the land beyond for at least a mile. Further up the coast, the shale was broken by a long rocky peninsula reaching far out into the rough Atlantic.

When he reached the shale ridges, Greycub stopped his hunting and ran at a steady trot behind them until he arrived at the peninsula. Once on it, he stuck very close to the rocky cliffs that dropped over fifty feet straight down to the sea until he came to a ruined cottage above the sea. This building had long ago been abandoned as the sea, eating chunks out of the cliff face, brought the place at last dangerously close to the very edge.

The wolf made his way through the ruin, but once on the other side looped back inland for half a mile and then, keeping to the roads as much as possible, galloped as fast as he could - straight back to the Hunter's house. And there, as dawn spread across the sky, cold and blond as the wolf's own flanks, he did a very strange thing indeed. He walked again along the little road that passed by the garden, following his own tracks of twelve hours before, and with a single, fleet leap, cleared the fence and landed lightly in the middle of an earthy rockery. Here, he sniffed about and walked to and fro a couple of times, leaving his prints in the soft earth between the stones. Then he stepped along the rocks embedded in the earth for several metres, leaving no tracks, before jumping back over the fence and into the road. This done, he trotted back behind the house, crept into the long grass again, that gave him a hidden view of the garden, and waited.

The two men were already stirring. Soon smoke rose from the chimney and the smells of cooking escaped from the kitchen. Greycub waited quietly behind the wall at the back of the house, his ears pricked for any movement outdoors.

After breakfast the guest departed. The Hunter came out, and stood and waved at the end of the drive while his friend drove away. Then he walked round behind the house and opened a door. Out came Jenny - old now, grizzled and more crooked than ever as her legs grew stiff and her old wounds hurt her, but with her nose as sharp as ever. Behind his wall Greycub stiffened; he did not want the little dog to find him, not yet. But the Hunter led her away to the lawn at the front of the house, away from him and his marks and scent. Jenny sniffed about the lawn while her master wandered to and fro, getting a breath of fresh air, before they both went back into the house. After an hour or so the Hunter came out again with Jenny, got into his car and drove off.

The Hunter took a walk round the garden every morning, while Jenny had her morning run. By sheer chance, that morning, and the following one, neither he

97

nor Jenny found the tracks that Greycub had left. Greycub moved himself from the long grass to a ditch further back, where Jenny would be less likely to find him. Day and night he lay still, not daring to venture out in case his new scent obscured the one he had laid down. There was a little water in the ditch, but nothing at all to eat. The wolf swallowed down his hunger; food was not important to him at this time.

On the morning of the third day the Hunter got up late, and did not arrive in the garden with Jenny until after nine o'clock. He was growing lazy, and began to think he must take his next expedition more seriously, before he grew soft. As he walked in the cool autumn morning around his little house, he spotted some flowers, gentians, blooming on the small patch of rockery near to the road. The Hunter had neglected the plants since he moved here, gardening was not his hobby. But he was pleased to see the pretty blue and walked over to have a look. Behind him, Jenny trotted, sniffing here and there and shaking her aching limbs.

As he stood looking at the little cluster of bright flowers, the little dog sniffed around the edges of the flowerbed. The Hunter watched her. Suddenly, she became electric. She sniffed here and there, rapidly, excitedly. The Hunter felt a thrill go through him. If Jenny was excited some prey must be near. But he was puzzled at the same time. There was nothing living in these parts that called for such excitement.

'What is it, girl?' he called softly. 'What have you found? Wildcat?'

Jenny looked up and whined. Then she crouched down on her belly, fawning and rolled over with her legs in the air. This was strange behaviour. 'What's wrong

98

with you?' he demanded. The little dog trotted away to one side and shook her head, yipping as if to call him. The Hunter ignored her but bent down to examine the ground where she had been. He stared at the prints for seconds without understanding what they meant.

'Wolf,' he said, without meaning to. He stood up.

The Hunter bared his teeth. The marks, three days old, half crushed by his own shoes, were still unmistakable to him. The dry weather had preserved them perfectly. He wondered what were they doing here, in his garden? The chance was so great he thought for a second that someone was playing a trick on him. But the print was no trick. He knew for certain that an English wolf had stood on this bank recently.

In the same second that the Hunter identified the print as wolf he recognised it as belonging to Greycub. Five years on and no longer just a cub, but he would have known Greycub's print anywhere. He was conscious of an itching sensation on the back of his leg where he had been bitten and still had a scar to prove it. Then he went inside, cut and packed some sandwiches, cut some meat for Jenny, swung a rifle over his shoulder, some rounds of ammunition in his pack, and locked up the house. He called Jenny over and took her to the scent. 'Track him,' he ordered. Jenny went down on her belly again, cringing as if she did not know what was expected of her. Cursing her stupidity, the Hunter grabbed her by the scruff of the neck and made her sniff the prints, but still Jenny refused to recognise what he wanted and ran to and fro, up and down, yipping and crying. But Greycub had not been cautious, and the Hunter could see by eye that the animal had left the garden and jumped out onto the road. Here there were tracks by the roadside, but confused tracks. It seemed the wolf had gone first one way and then another. But as he examined them Jenny seemed to understand what he wanted and wagging her tail and sniffing the ground, began at last to track. Evidently the wolf was not what his forebears had been. The Hunter could have followed these tracks by eye. It would be an easy hunt.

Man and dog followed along the road and off across the field the way Greycub had gone three days before. The hunt was on.

About half an hour after they had gone, the wolf rose from his lair beyond the garden and went round the house to the road. He lay out of sight for another half an hour by the hedge, then followed behind, checking with his nose that the Hunter was on his track.

The hunt was on.

Although there were many tracks, they were old, and it proved a slower business than the Hunter expected. Jenny was old; but still, she seemed to be taking longer than was necessary. The Hunter began to think of her strange behaviour when she found Greycub's tracks, and he remembered that she had actually tried to lead him away from them. He realised he had seen her act that way once before.

It was then that the Hunter linked her strange behaviour in the garden just now with her behaviour on the motorway, five years before, when Greycub had disappeared. Clearly, the cub had not been killed by a car. How then had he eluded Jenny's sharp nose? He looked at the little dog, so faithful to him all these years. Had she duped him? Had she betrayed him five years ago, and lost him his most wanted prize?

Now that they were on the track, Jenny seemed to have returned to normal. She made the odd mistake, but that was only natural in tracks as old as these - about four days old, the Hunter judged. Several times, they found themselves lost, but faithful little Jenny ran busily to and fro, and picked up the track again, and so the Hunter dismissed the doubts from his mind. Such thoughts - any thoughts - took away from the pleasure and intensity of the hunt. When at this work, his whole being was concentrated in his sense of sight - the way the grass lay; had it been crushed flat some time in the past few days, did it lie close to the ground? - the soft indentation in moss on the brickwork at the end of a ditch, the way the bracken was disturbed. These tiny signs, so slight that even he would not have made anything of them, had he not known there was a wolf about, became vivid, and seemed to flash out of the hedges, jump out of the grass at him. Thought was unnecessary. He became an animal of the eye.

By nightfall they were only just at the coast. The night was clear but dark under the thinnest sliver of moon. The Hunter could have trusted to Jenny's nose, but now that he had doubted her he decided to hunt by day and go no farther until the light returned.

He took out a sleeping–bag from his pack and wrapped himself up in it. He fed Jenny, ate some dried fruit and then brewed himself chocolate over a small primus stove. As he drank it on the edge of the beach before sleep, he allowed himself to speculate on the good turn his luck had taken that the animal he most wanted to destroy in the whole world had come to him in this way.

He recalled his feelings when he sighted the print on

the patch by the gentians. They would always be lucky flowers for him now. As he remembered, something came into his mind that had been floating uncomfortably about ever since his doubt about Jenny had first risen.

Those prints he had found outside the garden, on the roadside - there had been something odd about them - something he had been thinking about when Jenny began to track...

In his mind's eye, the memory of the prints was so clear he could study them in his imagination. Yes. The wolf had appeared to run first one way and then another, but now he could see this was not so. The difference was faint but unmistakable. He was certain. There were two sets of prints. His quarry had left the garden and returned hours later. Jenny was not leading him towards the wolf at all...

With a violent clarity the Hunter knew that Greycub was not ahead of him as he had thought but behind him. A cold breath blew on his neck; it seemed to him that the wolf even now sat behind him, the pink tongue and cruel teeth inches from his bare neck. His hair bristled, he shuddered and he turned himself slowly round to face - only the night. Quickly he slid his hand under his jacket and took out his hand gun. Jenny woke and came to lick his hand. He watched her, thinking, 'Traitor!' but saying nothing. He was no longer the Hunter but the prey. For the whole morning death had been close behind him and he had known nothing of it.

He did not sleep that night. He listened. But the wolf was clever. Perhaps he had seen the gun being drawn out from under his jacket. There was nothing all night.

As he kept his vigil he made his plans. This was to be no ordinary hunt. The normal situation, where the animal knew nothing of the killer on its track, was reversed. The wolf knew where he was and he had no idea where the wolf was. Not only that but his dog, his own little Jenny, was now not to be trusted. She could be leading him anywhere, even to his own death.

At this thought, and the idea that she had fooled him out of his prize five years ago, the Hunter wanted to shoot the little dog. But not yet. If he did that he would not have her nose to follow the track the wolf had laid down. He still needed her. The Hunter had one great advantage. He knew Greycub was behind him. He had no need to find the animal; he need only wait for the animal to find him.

'Tomorrow,' he whispered to himself.

The next day's hunting was the most uncomfortable he had ever experienced. He could not get rid of that sense of danger from behind. He felt those cool eyes on his back, imagined the animal sniffing at his tracks, knowing how far ahead he was, watching him from concealed places. Was the wolf a mile behind him or only a few metres? All the time he concentrated his eyes on the tracks ahead, his ears strained behind for the slightest crackle or hiss of breath, listening for a sudden rush of soft paws and the thud as the wolf launched itself at the back of his neck. This feeling was all the worse because he had to conceal his knowledge that the wolf was behind him. He did not want to lose his only advantage. Little Jenny sniffed so eagerly in bushes, wagged her tail, seemed to be enjoying the hunt. It seemed to him that she was laughing at him the whole time. Well, let her laugh. She would find out, in time...

At no point on his route was he able to look back

upon his path. Where he did cross open space, behind him was always a well-covered area, from which he could easily be observed without observing. And yet this never happened in reverse. In other words, the path they took was so designed that the wolf could often see him, but he could never see the wolf.

Only at one point did this arrangement fall through, when he reached the shale ridge that led to the peninsula. As he turned the corner to leave the mainland and go onto the peninsula he entered an area of dense short bushes, and from there was able to see a whole long stretch of open coastline, without himself being seen. Admittedly most of this was hidden by ridges of rock twenty or thirty metres up from the sea, but there was one small gap he noticed of perhaps five metres about half a mile from where the Hunter now stood. He knew the wolf had not yet crossed this gap, because to do so he would have to bring himself out into the open. Crouching concealed by the bushes, the Hunter would be able to watch the wolf cross this short space and so confirm his suspicions and get an idea of how far behind him the animal was.

Such a short space as five metres - and nearly half a mile away - would take the wolf a fraction of a second to cross at a run; the Hunter could miss it if he rubbed his eyes. He sat peering through the dense branches of the hawthorn bushes and waited. Jenny kept tugging at his clothes and whining, urging him on but he ignored her until at last she lay down and buried her nose in her paws. The warm sun could easily have made him drowsy after missing his sleep that night, but the excitement, and the chance of gaining the upper hand here kept him sharp and alert.

When it came it was even briefer than expected. A flash of gold and silver, nothing more, a snap of the fingers and it was gone. The wolf flew across that gap; it was impossible to get a clear look - it could have been a fox or a dog or a sunbeam shot from behind a cloud. But the Hunter knew.

All his fear was now gone. His knowlege was again superior, the wolf had become as clear as glass to him.

'You're dead,' he whispered to himself. He ran his eyes along the thin rows of ridges that approached to within a few metres of the bushes in which he hid. A long, wide smile spread over his jaws and remained there, even while his eyes, flickering over the terrain ahead, indicated that his pleasure was over and he was already plotting the circumstances of Greycub's death.

The Hunter's eyes rested on the point where the last ridge finally dipped out of sight into the earth. He could see his own footprints coming from behind it where he had followed the wolf; and now the wolf was following his tracks. There was every reason to suppose that within a few minutes, Greycub would emerge into the open at the same place. He would be exposed. He would go for the nearest cover - the very bushes in which the Hunter now hid.

In the few seconds it would take Greycub to cover that distance he would be dead. There was plenty of time. The Hunter need only be alert for the wolf's arrival. He admired the wolf for laying such a cunning plot, and he admired himself even more for so certainly finding the one point of weakness in it, the one moment when the wolf would be exposed.

It was to his advantage that the wind was in his face; the wolf would be unable to catch his scent. He took off his pack and placed the rifle on the ground before him. He would push himself into the bushes, lie on his belly and wait for the streak of gold that would certainly rush from behind the shale ridge, straight towards him.

But first there was a problem. Jenny was not to be trusted. She sat to one side, watching his preparations curiously, not wagging her tail now, he noted grimly, but whining under her breath.

'Here, girl, here Jenny,' he called. She did not come straight away and he lunged for her. She tried to run, but she was old and slow, and he had her by the collar. Struggling desperately, but not daring to growl, Jenny dug into the earth, frantically straining back, away.

'Little bitch,' he hissed, and took a sharp knife from his belt ...

The Hunter rested the barrel of his gun on a nobble of hawthorn root and settled himself into the ground. The ground was rough with roots and the stems of the hawthorns, and covered in dead shoots, sharp with thorns and spines. He noticed none of it. He expected Greycub in minutes. He calculated the wolf would fall dead about five metres in front of him, provided his first shot got him in the right place, as he was in no doubt it would. He could feel his mind sliding down the barrel of the gun, reaching along the line of sight, right down to the edge of the shale ridge. His whole being focused in this way. When the signal came his finger would move smoothly and discharge the little pellet of lead into the wolf's head. He regarded the animal as already dead. Nothing was more certain.

Chapter 14

Greycub had never been very far behind. Mostly he dropped back and followed the trail by scent, but every now and then he came within sight of the man. His behaviour was cautious, slow. He checked every step of the way with his nose on the ground and in the air; he listened and watched. When the Hunter camped on the beach he too had not slept, but waited, out of sight but within earshot of any activity, among the boulders scattered at the back of the beach. He did not bother stopping Jenny from catching his scent on the wind. He quickly realised that the little dog would not betray him. Once, while the Hunter was eating his lunch, she crept out of his sight and found the wolf hiding a hundred metres away in a young pine plantation. He let Jenny lick his lips and greet him, before sending her back to her place, by her master's side.

Later, Greycub stayed still in hiding behind some sea-smooth outcrops of rock halfway up the beach, as the Hunter made his way past the shale ridges. The ridges were not deep enough to hide a standing man, and Greycub peered out from behind the seaweedy clusters to check on his progress. From the same hiding place he watched as the Hunter left the flat, climbed the cliff and disappeared behind the hawthorn thicket.

As soon as the Hunter was out of sight he quickly slipped out from the rocks and jumped down behind the shale outcrops, where straight away he lay back down on the ground. There he waited five more minutes.

He rose, concealed by the ridges, and continued at a steady trot, a pace which he kept up all the way to the gap. Just before the gap he began to run, so that he hurtled past that space at speed, as the Hunter had noted; but once past he did not slow down. He kept up the same fierce pace until he reached a point where the sand dunes came close to the shore. Here, an undulation in the ground hid the wolf as he swerved to one side, still running as fast as he could go, and at right angles to his original track cut straight across inland.

Weaving between the dunes, keeping low to the ground, the wolf did not relax for several hundred metres. When he was sure he was out of sight he trotted on for a few minutes more, then he paused and began to sniff at the ground. He had found his own tracks where he had doubled back inland to the Hunter's house. Now he trotted along, but with no great signs of caution until he drew near to the broken cottage on the top of the cliff. There, he slowed right down. First, he crept downwind of it and sniffed the air. Then he crept on his belly up to his own tracks as he had approached the ruins from the other side, days before. There was no new scent alongside them. Still Greycub kept up his caution and crept by a devious hidden route right up within the ruins. Only then was he satisfied the Hunter had not come this far, and he turned his nose down to the headland.

The wind was in his face, and that was to his advantage as he could hear and smell any signs that his enemy was coming. He kept well to one side of his own tracks, checking every few metres or so that there was no one near him. When he finally came out above the hawthorn patch he stood and looked down. After the first glance he did not try and conceal himself. He could see the still form of the Hunter below him, see the thin steel of the murderous barrel. To one side of the Hunter was a bloody patch and there was Jenny, her throat cut, dead.

Greycub made no noise. He slid like a snake down to the edge of the hawthorn cluster. The soft thick grass, cropped close by rabbits, made no noise under his weight. He sniffed softly around and found the gap where the Hunter had forced himself through into the middle of the thicket. Greycub breathed in the close, fresh sweat of the Hunter, and slid inside.

The enemy lay oblivious to anything other than the barrel of his gun, which seemed to him to have an invisible spirit that reached down to the beach below. He expected the wolf to emerge any second. Greycub rustled the edges of the thorns as he entered the thicket, but the Hunter heard nothing, was aware of nothing but the focus of death in front of him. Even when the wolf lay down by his side, not more than a centimetre from his jerkin, he was unaware.

Greycub lay thus for a few seconds, like a dog by its master's side. Then he caught sight of the hand cradling the butt of the gun with one finger like a spring over the trigger. The wolf growled low and soft in his throat and reaching his head delicately to one side, took that hand in his jaws and crushed it down to the bones and through them.

So shocked was the Hunter and yet concentrating so powerfully ahead that he screamed as he lay there still waiting for the wolf to appear at the end of his barrel. When he realised where the animal was, he bawled in fear and tried to stand up and get the gun in its face, but the twigs that had hidden him now trapped him. They clawed at his face and caught the gun, pushed him back against them. He screamed again as the wolf almost casually reached out for the other hand, but missed and tore the rifle from the man's grasp instead.

Trying to protect his eyes as best he could the Hunter forced his way through the bushes, desperate to escape the wolf, who howled and roared at his side, tore at the flesh in the back of his legs. At last they burst out of the thicket and the Hunter ran, stumbling across the patchy grass. Within seconds he was at the cliff's edge; below the water foamed on the rocks; before him stood the wolf. The Hunter turned and leapt as far out as he could, praying he would miss the rocks, but preferring even them to the wolf's fury.

The water smacked into him and the shock of the cold stopped the pain for a minute. When he surfaced he was able to push away from the dangerous rocks and out into the clear sea. It was a still day, a calm sea. He held his breath, treading water and listening for the sound of Greycub swimming near him. But he was alone in the water; evidently the wolf did not like the cold sea.

The Hunter lay on his back, catching his breath. He forced himself to breathe calmly. It was not far to the shore, only a matter of twenty or thirty metres, but he knew for certain that the wolf would be waiting there for him when he came ashore, to finish the business. He had no gun, he was wounded. He would certainly be killed.

Not far offshore was a rock sticking out of the water and the Hunter swam over to it. Using his elbows he hauled himself half out of the water to view the shore. Greycub was already there, sitting by the water, watching him and waiting.

The Hunter lay half on the rock, half in the water. A small crab scuttled across the snails and weeds on the rock, waving its feelers in the water. It was late afternoon. Dusk was falling; it became dark very quickly in that northern climate and the water was so cold that the Hunter knew he could not survive for more than a few hours in it. He hung on the rock, watching the blood seeping out of his hand and clouding the water. It seemed impossible to escape. But he had already formulated a plan.

First he tried various means of moving through the water. He found that by lying on his back and gently kicking his feet, using his hands only as rudders, he could move with the least pain. It had the added advantage of being silent; the wolf would not be able to hear his progress, and since the wind blew onto the sea, the Hunter knew that once darkness was complete, he could move in the water without the wolf knowing which way he was going.

His only chance, he knew, was to find people. The wolf would not attack with other humans there.

There were two houses within a few miles of each other to which he could go for help. One, the nearer, lay in the direction they had come in, about two miles along the coast. The other, in the opposite direction, was only the same distance away were he on foot; but to swim to it he had to negotiate the peninsula and that put an extra three miles on the swim, through unknown currents.

Those three extra miles in his condition were terrible to consider. He was freezing cold, his hand was useless, he was still bleeding - the salt in the water kept the wounds open - and despite the clarity of his thinking, he was aware that somewhere inside was a deep shock from the savaging he had received, the nearness of death and perhaps above all, the fact that the wolf had defeated him in the hunt. He was fairly clear he could make one mile, close to the coast, although at a severe cost; but four, far out to sea, frightened him. He had made up his mind to take the easier option when a thought came to him. He remembered that his neighbour up the coast was away. The man had told him some weeks before that he had business in Edinburgh that week. He had no option but to go round the peninsula.

The Hunter's thoughts were disturbed by a tickling sensation on his hand. Looking down he saw that a dozen tiny crabs had crept out of the weeds and crannies and were picking at the flesh of his ruined hand with their claws. Already his hands were so numb he could barely feel them. He shouted and thrashed, so losing his hold on the rock and scraping skin off his arm as he scrabbled to get his head above water. He panted and clung weakly to his rock. Inland, he saw Greycub had stood up at his shout and was watching him closely. After a minute, he sat down again, his ears still pricked, to see what move his prey would make next.

Dusk was coming down fast. The Hunter had one last trick up his sleeve and now he played it. He played it despite the ordeal ahead, despite his pain. He pushed himself away from the rock and swam not around the peninsula but up the coast, as if he were going in the completely opposite direction. He swam this way, going out to sea as he did so, while dusk fell and then, quickly following, the night. Only when he was in deep darkness did he turn round and swim in the opposite direction, out to the tip of the peninsula.

He had been swimming twenty minutes and added half a mile and the best part of an hour onto his time in the water. But he had the satisfaction before the darkness fell and he turned round of seeing the wolf following him on the shore.

It was his good fortune to be swimming with the tides, but he still had to fight the swirling currents around the outcrop that threatened to drag him against the rocks and suck him under. He had to keep as far from the rocky feet of the cliff as he could. All around the peninsula there was no way of landing and in fact the house he was heading for sat on the edges of the first pebbly bay where it was possible for him to land. By the time, an hour later, he had reached the head of the peninsula he was deadly tired and had to keep resting, floating in the water, before the cold and fear of death forced him into movement. As he swam he kept looking to the cliffs above him, heavy and dark. But although the moon began to shed a little light between the clouds and the stars were bright, he could make out no shape following above him.

He considered at this point that his chances of survival were better than even. He had been pushed to the limits before, and he knew how far beneath the surface his strength ran. But he would be at the very end of his resources when he landed at the bay. Therefore, when, as he rounded the tip of the peninsula, a cold current grabbed him and forced him away from the rock and out into the deep waters of the open sea, he felt the beginnings of despair. He was unable to fight this current. For a while he hoped to go through and come out the other side, but after every few metres he was carried further away, his chances of life so much less. Finally he turned onto his belly and used his arms to swim. This did not hurt him so much as he thought. The cold water dulled his wounds. But when he reached the other side of the current and saw how far out of his way he had been carried his will almost failed. The effort had drained him and it seemed to him now that his limit had already been reached and passed, that the shock of the attack among the bushes was gaining on him and cold death was creeping up on him in the disguise of a friend. Better to drift and let the cold take him gently than fight and suffer pain, and worse, perhaps failure. He was still under halfway there.

On his back again he pushed death away, kicking his legs, fighting the cold, fighting his failing spirit, forcing himself back to the shore. It was another twenty minutes before he passed the peninsula's head. Now it was no longer him swimming, it was some other thing. His legs moved softly in the water, like dying fish. He could no longer feel his hands or even his arms.

Time slowed down. It ceased to matter how long it took him to reach the shore, so long as he kept on swimming, living, moving. The cold disappeared, or he could no longer feel it, and he knew this was a bad sign. He wondered if the dawn was near, but he'd lost all sense of time and he did not know that barely two hours had passed since he jumped into the sea. He could feel himself dying, but still he moved towards the bay, and life.

At last the shoreline was coming close. Every now and then he flopped onto his belly and soon he would see the little house stuck naked on the rocks just above the beach. He asked himself if it were a question of him surviving but losing his hands, did he want to live on those terms? The answer lay in his spirit; to his surprise he felt exultant. He had after all succeeded again. Always

114

before he had been the Hunter. Now he had been the prey and he had survived. He would live. He would kill again.

The next time he turned onto his belly, he could see the roof of the little house. A cry came out of his mouth, like a cawing - it sounded like an animal, he noted in surprise. But the animal was alive. He floated on his back and shouted again, trying to rouse the man from his bed.

Again he flopped over onto his belly. There was no light on and he was about to turn back over and yell again when he saw a dark shape move on the porch. For a second he hoped, but then he knew it was not a man. He froze in the water and started to sink. Then he began to shout and scream for that man, any man to come and help him, until he lost control and sank again, choking on the water. There was still no light. This neighbour too was away from home. He hoped desperately it was a dog he saw, but when the moon emerged from the clouds and he saw the pale flanks of the wolf, he knew he was a man with a choice of two deaths.

Undecided he drifted. Greycub walked down to the water to meet him, but the Hunter's will was paralysed with cold and defeat and shortly, when he fell into another current, he did not fight it but let it carry him out, back to the deep waters.